THE PATHS HOME

A Journey of Becoming

SARAH M. LOGAN

ISBN 13: 978-1546719212

ISBN 10: 1546719210

CHAPTER 1

How many animals he had at the zoo now, Cory wasn't sure as they were free to come and go. Some stayed, while others only came for one visit. Whether they came and went or came to stay, they enriched his life in countless ways. He wondered if he would ever know the extent of their help.

He had been strolling through the park-like estate and now stopped at the crest of the Japanese bridge to survey the vastness everything had become. Ahead of him, the baobab trees stood staunchly in a group and were a nice little walk from the bamboo grove with its paths that meandered through shadowed mazes of frothy leaves and stalks. Somewhere in the middle of them was the path that only sometimes he could find. It led to the spring that fed the lake he was standing above. Stretching out behind him a distance from the house were the forests of immense pines and deciduous hardwoods: the old growth forest and the new, young forest.

He leaned his arms on the lacquered rail and looked across the water through the hazy afternoon light to the low, lumpy hills. They were covered now in the apple greens of summer and in colors of the larger flowers: irises, daisies, and sunflowers. He couldn't see the multitudes of small, bright flowers hidden in the grass, but he knew they were there. In only a few months, the hills would slowly morph to gold, vermillion and a pumpkiny orange and then on to the alternating browns and whites of winter.

Past the hills, the desert baked under an endless sun and housed the cave that tunneled deep into the bluff at its western edge. Beyond it, well ... Cory didn't know what lay beyond the bluff. He'd never been that far.

He became aware of a woodpecker and was reminded that obstacles are illusions, a false sense of separation, an opportunity to help us reach our true goals, our true selves. He remembered when he had learned that and smiled at the memory. He sensed now that something was about to change again. That's okay, thought Cory. This lifetime is for change and for gaining experiences. He turned in a slow circle to memorize his surroundings, to remember what they were now before they changed again. To give himself a way to think about who he was now before he changed, too. It's all good, he thought as he took it all in. Everything is as it should be.

Throughout the estate, the birds and animals that had adopted him over the years went about their business. The first was with him still. Well, the first live animal—he counted Hank, his childhood stuffed lion, as the practice round for Daisy and the other living animals who followed. As he thought of Daisy, she flew onto his arm and looked up at him. Hopping off, she sat on the rail next to his elbow and viewed the hills with him. A simple, tiny chickadee. He had been so disappointed when she showed up so many years ago.

The memory was still vivid. They'd been reading fables and fairy tales in school, and their teacher explained the role of helper animals in the stories. Everyone thought that was cool and assigned animals to themselves and to each other. He had chosen a lion, of course, and been assigned an alligator by his friends. He liked those. They were manly and tough. His friends nicknamed him Gater, and he tried to live up to it.

The Paths Home

Then, Daisy showed up in his back yard and at his window. He didn't recognize her at first, but she was relentless. She started showing up at the playground and everywhere else he went. He knew it was the same bird because of the way she acted and looked. He didn't know what kind of bird she was, but he did know she wasn't cool like a lion or alligator.

One day, though, he just got it. People really can have helper animals, but they choose you. So, he first looked carefully at her as she ate the seeds he'd put in the window feeder. He then looked through a bird book he had checked out from the library. Comparing each picture to her, he finally found her—a chickadee, a plain, ordinary chickadee. An animal for a girl. He did not tell his friends, who continued to call him Gater.

But something drew him to her. He named her Daisy, sometimes calling her Dais or Daisychain. When he saw her, he'd go outside to talk to her. Soon, he began looking for her even on the ball field and outside his classroom. It didn't take long for her to come to his whistle and to recognize the name he'd given her.

When the weather started to cool, he built her a birdhouse and placed it out of the wind and near his bedroom window. His dad came home one Wednesday in late fall and said they were supposed to have record cold over the weekend. He looked at Cory and offered to help him convert his bedroom window to an indoor/outdoor aviary. Cory's eyes lit up. He hadn't realized his dad had noticed. Did he want it for his birthday present, his dad had asked. He said, yes, very much. Good, his dad had said because he'd ordered one, and it had been delivered.

They spent the next two evenings building and installing it. Daisy sat on the birdfeeder and looked interested. When it was ready, Cory sprinkled a trail of seed from the outside part to the inside, but Daisy didn't need that as enticement. She flew straight in and hopped around, found the water dish and the nest, and made herself at home and stayed.

His friends had started to notice her following Cory around and began teasing him. They quit calling him Gater. By that time, Cory didn't care. In fact, even sports held less interest for him. Some continuing ed classes at the university, that allowed teens with a teacher's permission, had captivated him. His English teacher was happy to write the required letter, and he enrolled. The classes were taught by a professor who was excited about his subject matter and his students' learning and who made sure Cory was not left out. It was probably that professor who started him on his life's work as keeper of a special zoo. He'd always thank him.

Daisy pecked very gently at his elbow. "Ow, Dais, that kind of hurt," said Cory coming out of his reverie and looking down at her. She cocked her head at him, *I was gentle and you aren't a wimp.* "You were gentle," said Cory petting her feathers with one finger. "Sorry, Daisychain, I'm just a bit antsy. I heard the woodpecker. Are we going somewhere?" She hesitated and then flew off towards the desert. Cory sighed. He could tell it was the desert and not the hills. He didn't like the desert.

He knew nothing there could hurt him unless he let it, and the only animals there were his animals. But it wasn't as pleasant as the hills with their flowers or the forest of birches with their papery bark or the lake with its little inlets and islands that were home to frogs and water birds. In the forest, he could occasionally spot a fawn or a badger, and he loved looking for ducklings at the lake. He could happily spend a day quietly walking or rowing and watching for his animals, but where Daisy led, Cory followed. He straightened his back and stepped down from the bridge. Stopping home briefly, he started making his way towards the desert.

CHAPTER 2

By late afternoon, Cory reached the desert's eastern edge. At least, he wasn't going to be greeted with a whole day of heat, but he would quickly be faced with night. He knew about night in the desert and what it asks of a person, especially if the desert belongs to that person. However, he had everything he'd need in the canvas bag he had picked up before starting out. He looked around. No Daisy. She wasn't about to sleep rough, but then again it wasn't her calling. She and the woodpecker were just the callers. She'd show up if he needed her.

He scouted around for a place to spend the night. He knew parts of his desert well, but he'd entered at a different point, and it took him some time of walking and looking to find a depression with a few trees, which meant a water source. He gathered a number of small rocks and started scooping sand and pebbles until he got a bubbling of water. He made a rock ring to hold the water in a small pool and hung a hammock between two palms. Before doing so, he peered into the fronds. Yes, there were coconuts growing above. Good, maybe he could get one in the morning.

Cory laid out the food he'd brought, asked a blessing, and ate as the sun set. When it was almost at the horizon, he turned his whole attention to its setting. In the desert, the sun does not take a lazy stroll towards the horizon. It sinks as if drowning. Cory wanted to make sure he did not miss the sinking as it marked the entry into night. The shadows of the palms lengthened, reaching out to him and then covering him, and with that, night, inky black at first. As Cory's eyes adjusted to the lack of light, stars seemed to pop from the darkness until they made their own shadows. This is what Cory had been waiting for.

He went and rummaged in his bag. Finding a tiny pool of light, he sat and looked over the small pouch he'd retrieved. He had made the entire thing. He grew the cotton, picked and combed it, spun it, weaved it, and, finally, cut the cloth and sewed it into a pouch with knitted, draw-string closure. He had even embellished it with leftover pieces of cotton thread he dyed. His embroidery wasn't all that pretty, but it was meaningful.

Turning the pouch over in his hands several times as he relived the experience of its making, Cory looked at his work. He stroked a finger over several of his favorite designs and then over his least favorite. Making the pouch had been a changing point in his life, and, as usual, Daisy had inspired it. Cory gently shook its contents into one hand and then smoothed the pouch against his leg before laying it to one side. There was no breeze, but he laid a small rock on top of it in case one sprang up. After all these years, he did not want to lose it.

He picked through the contents, the mementos he'd collected over his life. Some he'd made. Others he'd found or been given. Only one had material worth. All reminded him of who he had been and who he was now. He knew the purpose of this desert visit was to add one more for where he was heading. When it would find him or where, he did not know yet. He did know he would spend as much of the night as he needed to prepare himself for its discovery.

Closing his eyes and opening the hand that held his treasures, Cory picked one at random. Funny how his fingers

The Paths Home

always found this one first. It was a tiny, crudely carved bird, a chickadee. There was no way to tell it was a chickadee, and anyone else might not even realize it was a bird except for the outlines of wings on the sides and a stub of a tail sticking out at the back. Cory had wanted to commemorate Daisy's first year with him and had carved it for her. When he showed it to her, she had cocked her head one direction and then the other and then fluttered over to a snack of suet and chopped raisins he'd made her for an anniversary treat. No matter. Even into adulthood, Cory counted it as his most prized possession. Without Daisy, he wasn't sure who he might have become.

He set the carving on the flattened pouch and reached for another. When his fingers closed around a small, clear-plastic case, he smiled. He did not open the case. What lay inside was too delicate. Hoping to see the colors, though, he held it in the little pool of light, but there wasn't enough yet.

He closed his eyes and remembered how he'd found the little feather. Walking one day in the woods in a sprinkle of rain, he'd heard screeching and whining and yelps. He walked as quickly and quietly as he could towards the sounds. A young badger was trying to get at a blue jay fledgling that was flapping ineffectively on the ground. Cory stood at a distance and watched. Mama jay circled her offspring and made aerial attacks on the badger, who tried to make dashes at the baby bird. The baby was squawking and flapping, getting a little altitude just to return to earth. This went on for a time until a large clap of thunder preceded a downpour. The badger admitted defeat and scuttled for a burrow as the blue jay ushered her fledgling into thick undergrowth.

Cory had gone back the next day, but there was no sign of them. The rain, which had not let up, had erased any tracks. Only a tiny, downy feather caught on a low branch of a birch suggested they had been there. Too high for the badger to reach, the branch gave Cory hope the baby had made it.

Good, the badger could have something else for its dinner. He gently disentangled the feather, bright blue at the quill and white at its tip. He folded it in a piece of paper for safekeeping until he could get it home. A badger later adopted him as did a jay. He liked to think it was the same badger and baby he had seen that day. He had not seen either in a long time, but their lessons stuck with him still.

Opening his eyes, he placed the feather near the carving. Before reaching for another remembrance, he looked up into the sky. The moon had begun to rise, and the desert air was beginning to get cold. He made a protective fist around the remaining objects and got up to get his hoody from where he'd left it in the hammock. He glanced longingly at the hammock but went back to his task. He laid each object on the pouch after spending some time remembering its finding and its lessons.

Finally, only one object remained. He sighed. It was almost always the last one he picked. He didn't know if it was because he could feel its weight or shape or because it was the only one with material value. Or, because it had cost him dearly. With the moon's rise, there was now enough light to see the blue jay feather's delicate colors and certainly enough to see the ruby ring he was holding. He lifted it between his thumb and index finger and held it to the light where it glowed from within a deep, clear crimson. The circle of diamonds around it sent out their own tiny fires.

He sat for a few minutes unwilling to bring up the memory even though he already felt the stabbing in his chest as he had that day. He went back to an earlier, happier memory, but it had long been tainted by the final encounter. He let out his sigh and forced himself to look at both memories again. They did change over time, and maybe this time he could get through them and give them at least some peace.

He started with the earlier memory and decided to recite it aloud. Feeling a bit silly, he told the story to the ring. "I wore the shirt she liked best, the one in blue and white checks. I even ironed it, and I got my hair trimmed. I had the box in my pocket. When I picked her up, she said I looked especially nice. I thought that was a good sign." He smiled ruefully. "We wandered through the midway, shared a cotton candy. We rinsed our fingers in a water fountain. I then suggested a ride on the merry-go-round and made an excuse to get her to sit in the swan boat with me instead of on her own horse. After the ride started moving, I turned towards her and pulled out the box and proposed. She said, yes. We kissed, and the riders around us all clapped. The day was sunny and bright. Everything was perfect."

Cory stopped unable to go on. Knowing he had to or do this all again at some future date, he grasped the ring more firmly and continued. "It was only after we started planning a life together that it became obvious she didn't share my goals or values. For some reason I'll probably never understand, she made up her mind that the zoo should be a tourist attraction." He paused. "The first time I invited her to see it, I explained carefully that this zoo was different, not a place people come to look at animals, but a place of rest and renewing for the animals." Cory shook his head. "I thought I just needed to explain again."

At this point, the memory took on a life of its own. It was as if Cory was outside it looking on at someone else's story. The ring felt warm, almost hot, in his hand. Neither of these things had ever happened before. He watched the story unfold. He could almost hear the story as if someone was reading it from a book: So, Cory explained again, and then he explained differently. He told her about helper animals and how they choose us and that his zoo—as he liked to call it—was their safe place and that his job was to provide that for them. He thought she understood, but she didn't.

He started reciting the story along with the invisible reader: "She started working on him almost daily. She said the zoo should have a carousel to commemorate their love and row boats so people could go out to enjoy the lake. She wanted him to add rides and vendors, and, of course, cage the animals. It was when she said that, he knew. 'I can't cage the animals,' was all he could think to say. 'I won't,' he added. 'How can we work this out?'" In the memory, Cory stood still and waited for her answer. In the desert, Cory, too, waited, knowing the outcome but not wanting to see it. He watched but no longer recited.

She pulled the ring off and handed it to him, sneering as she did so, and walked away. That's what hurt the most, the sneer that said he was stupid, that he was nothing. And for a while he thought maybe she was right, for how had he missed all the signs of who she truly was? It had taken him a long time to realize he was something and longer to forgive himself.

"I forgive myself," Cory said softly to the ring. He opened his eyes, blinking away tears, and looked around. There, gathered on the desert, were all his animals. The blue jay sat next to the badger watching him, a fawn inspected the remains of his dinner, two ducklings tested the pool he had made. He could feel the rest of them ringed around him. It was a good feeling knowing he had done right by them. He could no more cage them than he could cage himself. He said, "Thank you," and this time, he felt he had perhaps made it through these two memories.

He placed the ring with the other objects and looked at them. Twenty-some years were represented in these reminders of who he'd been and who he might be. Twenty-some years of living and learning about the infinite and eternal, about God, and about where he, Cory Waters, fit in the grand plan of everything. He wondered what the new object would be and began the second part of his preparation.

CHAPTER 3

Cory carefully placed his mementos back in the pouch and put it back in his canvas bag, which he tied to the hammock. He was about to go back and clean up the remains of his dinner when he felt eyes staring at him. He turned slowly not wanting to startle whatever was there and saw a coyote sitting in the shadows. He'd not met this animal before. He knew Coyote can be a trickster and hoped this one wasn't. He was tired and just wanted to make a small fire and meditate. He said hello and, pointing to the rest of his dinner, offered it. The coyote stood and went over to sniff it. "Sorry there's no meat." The coyote delicately pulled a piece of cheese off the napkin and took it a little way off to eat. "There's water over here," Cory offered. The coyote looked but didn't seem interested.

Cory made his small fire and sat down by it. He closed his eyes and was about to begin his mediation when he felt a body next to him. He looked down and saw that the coyote had lain down near him as a dog might. "I'm naming you Ralph," he said. "So, Ralph; you are welcome to stay, but I'm going to sit here and meditate for a while." Ralph grunted, licked a foot and closed his eyes.

Cory resettled himself and began by taking stock of what he'd accomplished. He knew he'd been fortunate throughout his life, first, in finding his life work early, for he knew as a boy what that would be. He graduated from college and got a master's degree in zoology—that always made him laugh—and then the apprenticeships and various positions in several countries and at various institutions until he felt qualified to look after the entire operation himself. He moved on to where he was now: alone but not lonely, healthy, materially secure, blessed with a handful of good friends and family—people who loved him just because he was Cory. He felt fulfilled in his work but had recently begun feeling the need to extend himself in a new, and as yet unknown, direction.

He glanced at the hammock and then back at the fire. He stretched and heard Ralph grunt again. A lot like a pet dog, he thought, but not ever to be expected to be that and certainly not trusted to be his best friend in the traditional sense. He settled into his meditation. As he let the flames talk to him, he suddenly knew what was being asked of him. He got up, picked up the bit of litter he'd made, untied the hammock, repacked everything in the bag, made sure his water bottle was full, and said, "Come on, Ralph. Show me what you have for me."

Ralph opened one eye, got up, shook his fur back into place and sauntered off in a westerly direction. His pace was slow enough that Cory could follow without worrying about turning an ankle on an undetected stone. The moon seemed to strengthen, and the desert came alive with its soft light. They walked for some time, Cory simply keeping Ralph in view. Most of the time that wasn't a problem as the coyote strolled a few steps ahead of him. Several times, though, he took off at a gallop.

The first time it happened, Cory was sure he'd been tricked into venturing out into the darkness for what purpose he wasn't sure. He knew nothing too awfully bad could happen to him in his own desert unless he let it, but still. He stopped, not wanting to venture too far, and remained standing hoping Ralph would come back. After a couple of minutes and no Ralph, he tested the ground for rocks or a thorn bush and sat down to wait. He tried to look around, but it was too dark to see anything but shadows. He had counted on Ralph to take him where he needed to go. Perhaps he had been gullible. He stopped and felt. No, not gullible, he decided. Everything felt right. There was a different purpose.

Not able to see anything around him, he looked up. The recent clouds had moved off, and the moon was now strong. He let its light comfort him and began to think about the difference between sun and moon. The moon reflects, he reminded himself. It can only give off what the sun gives it. If the sun were to forget or refuse, the moon couldn't do its job.

"I've been so blessed and so stupid," Cory said softly. "First, He will never leave me or the moon or any of us without His light. Second, our jobs are to reflect that light." Then, the thought struck him, and he swallowed hard. I wonder what I've forgotten or refused to do. "Please," he whispered. "I don't want to forget anything You want me to do, and I certainly don't want to refuse."

Cory pondered what all this might mean in a person's life. What should I reflect? How should I reflect? How can I know I'm doing my job and not refuse something I don't know I'm refusing? He reminded himself that he had to stop and search for the feeling that told him what he was doing, or even thinking, was right and good. Not just what he wanted but right and good in a much larger sense even if he was uncomfortable with it. And then he had to go do whatever it was even if it was a bit scary. Then he thought, not refusing is easier than remembering.

Cory was getting himself in a muddle. "I guess just doing something even if I don't want to is still easier than resolving to do something and in thinking it, forgetting to actually do it." Somehow it all made sense, better sense in thinking it than in trying to put it into words. "Help me remember," he said and knew the infinite and eternal, his angels and God would know what he meant. The moon shone on, the night continued to be a dark blankness, and the coyote did not return, but Cory smiled for he had gained invaluable insight. He felt, he knew, everything was as it should be. He pulled out the hammock, wrapped it around himself and using the canvas bag as a pillow, fell sleep.

He was rudely awakened by a large, wet nose. Forgetting his guide was a coyote, he jumped not sure what had touched him. He opened his eyes to see two yellow eyes peering back at him. *Nice nap? Come on. We have places to go.*

It was still dark. Cory checked the moon. He had probably only gotten a half hour or so of sleep, but he felt refreshed. He packed the hammock and said, "Lead on." Ralph wheeled around and sauntered off but now in a more southerly direction. Cory didn't think he'd been in this part of the desert. Of course, it was difficult to tell without being able to see it properly, but it felt new.

Ralph trotted off a few more times and each time Cory took a short nap or at least a rest. The time Ralph came back looking smug, Cory asked, "Nice dinner?" Ralph ignored that but looked as if he'd been caught at his own game. This was also the time that instead of sauntering on, Ralph sat down and looked at Cory until Cory sat down. Ralph was facing east, so Cory skootched himself around and looked east, too. The faintest hint of color was entering the sky. When the light became enough to see by, Ralph stood up.

Cory had been thinking and didn't at first notice. When he did, he struggled to his feet. Stiff with the long periods of walking and lying on hard ground, he had to unkink himself before he could accomplish it. When he was finally up, Ralph gave a call. So, that's what coyotes sound like. Cory thought he knew how their calls sounded, but this was different. After calling, Ralph searched the air to the west. Cory looked, too, but couldn't see anything out of the ordinary. Ralph seemed intent, however. Assuming coyotes can see a whole lot better than he could, Cory waited patiently.

After what seemed like a half hour but was probably only five minutes, Ralph sat down, scratched an ear, and looked at Cory and held his gaze. Finally, Cory said, "I understand. Thank you, Ralph. You were a good guide." Ralph dipped his head and made his final departure; Cory waited.

CHAPTER 4

He remained standing but walked around to keep himself limber. One boot skidded on something, and he looked down. Gleaming against the darker background of grays and tans was a small, bright yellow pebble. Cory smiled. He didn't think this is what he'd come to the desert to find, but it would be nice to have a remembrance of Ralph. He bent over, much more smoothly now, and picked it out from among the other pebbles. He brushed off a few grains of sand and pocketed it. This pebble wasn't for the pouch, but he liked the comfort of taking Ralph along with him. It might not make it home; it might only make it to his immediate destination, but either way was fine: home with him or home where Ralph needed to be.

Looking back toward the west, Cory felt a presence coming towards him but still could not see it. He didn't want to start in a direction until he was sure of the direction he should go, but when another five minutes went by and nothing seemed to happen, he continued south but modified it to southwest. Even in his uncertainty, Cory soon felt he'd made the right decision. The land had lightened and had absorbed the reds, oranges and purples of the sunrise. The day was fresh, and walking was pleasant. He looked around at the terrain of undulating sand and pebbles. No trees or bushes broke the monotony.

Midmorning, he stopped to drink. In hooking his water bottle back onto his belt, he looked down. His shadow, long and thin, stretched out in front of him. He noticed another, much smaller shadow at his right shoulder. It looked like a magic wand moving on its own. Turning, Cory saw a bumble bee bouncing near him. Only momentarily startled, Cory knew this is who he had been expecting.

He lifted his hand to the bee, who made a smooth landing into his palm and walked around. Well, thought Cory. I've learned to communicate with lots of different animals including a praying mantis, but I've never had a bee. His hand was getting uncomfortable palm up. He slowly rotated it to a better position. The bee walked sedately up his thumb and settled there.

Once Cory recognized an animal as a helper, he named it. "Zanzibar" popped into his head. "I don't know what others call you, but I'm going to call you Zanzibar. Zanzi, for short," he told the bee. This didn't seem quite right. "On second thought, not Zanzi. It doesn't suit you." Zanzibar walked up and down Cory's thumb. It tickled, but Cory remained still.

"So, Zanzibar, I'm following you." The bee sat there. He didn't seem like an indecisive bee, so what was going on? Finally, Cory started slowly walking. Zanzibar turned around so he was facing the direction they were headed. Cory asked, "This way?" No answer, not even a buzz or a flit of wings, just the slightest of feelings that Cory was making the right decision.

They continued like this for much of the morning: Cory walking, stopping and feeling, correcting direction a bit if he needed to, but basically heading south-southwest, and Zanzibar perched and silently guiding. Cory tried once to suggest that Zanzibar sit on his shoulder as his arm was getting tired. He rotated his hand and placed it against his collarbone. Zanzibar moved from Cory's thumb to the back of his hand but either sat on his index finger or walked around. Cory finally gave up and put his hand out front again. He did shift his bag to his right shoulder so he could rest his elbow on it. That eased his arm, and Zanzibar settled on his thumb again, seemingly content and definitely in charge.

As he walked, Cory let his mind relax. His thoughts flowed smoothly without much help from his conscious mind. He had assumed when Daisy indicated he was to head to the desert, and Ralph headed west, that he would be going into the cave at the western end, but that didn't seem to be where they were heading. He wasn't sure how he felt about that. He'd never been in the cave, and he both eagerly looked forward to when he would be invited and anxiously hoped it wouldn't be soon.

Zanzibar bumped his thumb. It was far short of a sting, just a pay attention sort of bump. Cory stopped day dreaming and looked around. It was still just sand, pebbles, a few thorn bushes and rocks, sky and sun, but ahead the land rose. Cory realized it was late morning, nearing noon. Only a little shade remained. He found the largest bush and sat in its tiny pool of shade. Zanzibar flew onto a long thorn, and turned to Cory. Cory nodded and said, "I'll eat my lunch and then follow after you."

He watched Zanzibar's flight to mark the direction: yes, towards the distant rise. He then rummaged in his bag and pulled out a large handkerchief along with his leftovers. Taking off his cap, he covered the sides and back of his head and let the cloth flow freely, holding it in place with the cap. He adjusted the cap's back strap to the added thickness and unwrapped his lunch. He was more thirsty than hungry and more tired than thirsty, but he knew he needed to eat, and he wasn't about to fall asleep without shade for protection.

That's funny, he thought. We think of living in sunshine as being good but living in shade as a lesser existence when, really, too much sun just burns us out and shade offers a rest and a chance to renew. I'm sorry I thought I'd rather go to the lake or the new forest. The desert has taught me so much already, and it's not been as difficult as I thought it would be and not nearly as difficult as going to the cave would have been.

The short break was enough to strengthen him and as all shade was now gone, Cory started up again. He immediately stopped though and said a short prayer for what he still needed to learn. After a moment, he also pulled the yellow pebble from his pocket. "You belong to the desert, Ralph. I'm not sure where I'm heading or what's over that rise, but if it's not more desert, then I don't think you'll be happy there. Thank you for your good guidance and help." He placed the pebble under the thorn bush and started towards the rise. He only looked back once not even sure why. Nothing looked different. As he turned to start again, the thought descended to him, but everything is different now. The new is coming.

CHAPTER 5

The heat was stifling and the sun relentless. Cory hoped the rise wasn't a mirage. Zanzibar had not returned, and Cory was worrying that he'd misunderstood the bee's instructions. He hadn't been walking all that long since his lunch break, but his lack of sleep and the excitement and anxiety were taking their toll. His pace slowed, and he stumbled. Stop, just stop, he told himself. "I need a little help here," he said aloud. Nothing seemed to happen; nothing seemed to change. He blinked and looked around. The rise was ahead, the desert behind. The path ahead looked hard. He could just turn around and go home.

His thinking was getting fuzzy, but he remembered something Daisy had taught him years earlier when he had had to choose between her and the friends who wanted him to do their things but not his. "They aren't really friends, are they, Daisychain? Not if they want me to give up being me to please them."

Cory was about to start up again when his thoughts didn't feel finished, and he began to realize the oddness of asking for help and receiving that particular memory. Then he chuckled and shook his head. I'm my own worst enemy. Towards the rise is the way I should keep going, the way I truly want to go, not back to my house ... to do what? Let that part of me that wants me to give up win? He shook his head at his own forgetfulness. And it had been only, what, a few hours ago that he had asked help to always remember? Well, he had gotten the help he asked for. "Thank you," he whispered and knew everything was okay.

Cory slowed his breathing and pretended Daisy was with him. How silly, of course she was—she always was—and, as she'd taught him, he looked within himself and found strength to keep going. To his surprise, he also found a world he had not known existed there. He was barely touching that world consciously, but he found his feet were moving, and soon, he was bending his knees as the land rose. He came back into himself and applied his mind and will to the task of climbing the rise. The hill was steeper than it looked from below.

Cory soon quit trying to climb straight up and began to zigzag. "Like a bee," he laughed. He wondered if Zanzibar would come back. He hoped so. He was getting rather fond of him. He hoped he could meet his family and see his home. What was he thinking? He didn't even know if Zanzibar was a he. He might be a she, and she might be the queen, and then Cory would be meeting a whole hive, and that would be just a bit scary. He didn't know bee etiquette. He didn't want to get stung.

The final pull up the dune seemed almost vertical. Cory wondered if he was up to it. He almost decided again this wasn't what he was supposed to be doing after all. He looked within himself for direction and thought about the world he had just found and the strength he continually found if he looked. It was a quiet strength that took a bit of effort to find, but he always found it in time. He then thought about the story of Jacob and the angel. Instead of being led by a peaceable coyote, he could have had to wrestle him all night.

I'm still upright and walking. I haven't had to crawl across the desert. I certainly haven't had to wrestle anything except myself. I've only had to break a sweat. This isn't that difficult. Cory talked to himself in this way as he zigzagged back and forth in increasingly longer arcs that took him slowly up. He stopped, planting his lower foot for stability, and looked behind him. Painted on the slope below were the tracks of his crossings. He looked ahead. The top was just above him. So near.

He decided it would now be faster to crawl. He secured his bag around his shoulders and dug his hands into the sand and started to claw. He closed his eyes against the sand he was kicking up. He could feel it slipping by his hands and the dig of pebbles into his palms, and rocks, some with sharp edges, scraping the backs of his hands. It only seemed to take moments, and Cory was at the top. Too tired to stand, he lay where he was and then squinted down the other side. It looked to be all sand, no rocks. A small tree near where the land flattened offered some shade. He closed his eyes.

Cory halfway rolled and halfway skidded slowly downwards until he could feel the hill flatten and the temperature drop. He put out a hand and felt bark and coolness around the tree's trunk. He lay there until his breath returned and then said a short thank you for the trip thus far. Even the hard parts didn't seem that bad now. He felt the slightest of touches and then fuzzy hairs tickling his hand, and he smiled. "Hello, Zanzibar. Glad to see you again."

Cory opened his eyes and sat up. He surveyed the scratches on his hands. Zanzibar seemed concerned. "It's okay," said Cory. "Just a few scratches from the pebbles and sand." Zanzibar still didn't seem to like it. Cory felt he should put his hands out, so he did. Several bees he hadn't noticed landed gently on the backs of his hands and walked around leaving a balm of what, Cory didn't know. More bees joined them. I'm meeting the hive! thought Cory.

His hands were covered in bees. He had to resist the urge to flap them off and take care of the scratches himself. Without being told, Cory slowly turned his hands palms up. A new group of bees traded places with the others and walked around on his palms leaving their balm as the others hovered nearby. The entire process only took a few minutes, and then all but Zanzibar flew off. Cory looked at his hands. Where there had been scratches, some of them angry looking, there was a thin coating of bumble bee ointment. Cory looked closely. Some of the smallest scratches were almost gone and the redness of the worst was fading. "Thank you," he said to Zanzibar. "Please thank them all for me."

He took a long drink from his water bottle and noticed it was starting to get low, so he didn't take a second. He looked around. Everything was still sand, sun and sky, but a few trees dotted the land now. He felt renewed enough to start walking again. In putting a hand down to get his feet under him, Cory felt something hard and knobby. He brushed the sand aside until he uncovered what his hand had touched.

It continued to surprise him the things he was finding in his own desert. Things he had no idea were there. He wondered how long he had carried these things around with him: the good and the ugly, the useful and the useless. He wondered about the inner world he had tapped earlier and resolved to spend time soon, this evening maybe, exploring it.

Reaching his fingers into the sand, he plucked out a conch shell. The same yellowish tan, it was undetectable by sight and so small it would fit comfortably in a small child's fist. He sat back down under the tree to look at it. How did it get here to this part of the desert? What was it doing here with no ocean nearby? What did it mean that it was here?

He looked up finally and then all around, and his heart sank. He didn't know where Zanzibar was. "Zanzibar?" No answer. Did he think Cory was walking again? Had he truly missed the bee's cues this time? "Zanzibar!" No answer still. Cory felt his energy stream away. His muscles felt weak and his will was nonexistent. It was, for the moment, all too much, and Cory took the hammock out of his bag, made a pallet out of it and fell asleep.

And had a dream. He was walking in his desert. It began to rain, a straight-down, drenching rain. He took his hat and handkerchief off and let the rain soak him and clear the dust and sweat of traveling from him. Flowers started popping in full bloom from the sand. Everywhere he looked, the sand was being covered in blues and whites and greens. Soon, almost all the sand was hidden, and Cory found himself walking through masses of calf-deep flowers. "But I don't want to trample them," he begged, and a tiny path of cobblestones appeared in front of him. Wherever he stepped, stones appeared just before he put a foot down. The flowers were safe, and Cory could walk unhindered, without sorrow.

He stopped and looked down to his feet and then past his feet to mountain ranges underneath: hidden fairy realms, something out of Tolkien. Cory could see a whole world as if through a watery mirror. It was a world with its own terrains and life and sun but all in reverse. He looked back up at his desert and saw through what was there to its hidden life of mountains and valleys, sun and mists, castles and huts. The sand reflected the gold of the sun, but behind that façade, Cory could see the abundant life of a more temperate climate and beneath that, a vast ocean of water and stars: the cradle. Cory realized his desert contained immeasurable fields and an ocean, maybe more than one, and it always had. He just hadn't known it.

This was Cory's world within, the world he had discovered earlier in the day when he thought Zanzibar had deserted him. "This is all in me?" he whispered. He was awed

Sarah M. Logan

and stopped. The dream stopped; time and space stopped. Cory saw it all, felt it all, was it all. *I have a lot to do*, he thought, and everything started up again. He came back to the ocean which gave way to the field and then the desert, but before the last flower disappeared into the sand, a small conch shell fell into his open palm. Looking up into the searing desert sky, Cory saw a hawk circling away from him and heard it call as it passed. "I'm to follow the hawk."

Cory woke up when soft, fuzzy legs walked across his nose and forehead. He sat up and put his hand out. Zanzibar flew onto it. "I'm glad you're back," he said. *Let's have a conversation.* "Okay." *What have you learned?* "I have a lot to do and no time to carry with me what's no longer useful." *So, where do you go now?* "To the ocean," Cory said firmly, "to learn about its depths. To learn about all depths: those eternal, the ones that are infinite, God's." *They will carry you for the rest of your life.* "I'm not that old, and I have a lot more life left, I hope." *It's a very big ocean, and God, well He's infinitely larger than you can ever imagine.*

Zanzibar got up as if to say we're starting. "Just a moment, please," said Cory. Zanzibar sat back down. "I want to put the conch shell in the pouch." *No need.* "What? I thought it's what I came for." *You came for something else.*

Cory put the pouch away and, placing the shell in his shirt pocket, started walking away from the dune and towards the ocean. Zanzibar didn't have to tell him the direction. Cory just knew. Soon, as if for confirmation, the smell of salt water reached him. He followed it and the cry of a hawk. He could still hear him although he could not see him. In fact, for the rest of his life, he heard a hawk in moments of recentering and redirection.

Towards sundown, Cory crested a small rise, and there was the ocean: blue and green and white. He could feel the life in it. It mirrored the life within himself. He suddenly realized he wanted to paint it, but he was no painter.

A small cabana and hut awaited him. He changed into swim trunks and ran into the waves. Splashing and shouting joyfully with abandon, he stopped to watch the sun slowly glide to the ocean's western edge where it lingered to send out the warmest of colors across the ripples. Too soon, it disappeared under the water at the edge of the world. The moon rose silently, a pale yellow, and relit the sky in a much softer glow.

Cory had brought the food he found in the cabana out onto the beach and was eating and watching the sky, finding constellations, and breathing in the cool breeze. He lay down to see the sky better and to think about his next steps. His choices had brought him to this place, but now what was he supposed to do? He thought again of the cave at the desert's western edge. He could just make it out from where he was. He considered his choices. I didn't know it was this far south. I'll bet it's no more than an hour's walk, which means it's probably more like two, but still, I'd be walking mostly along the beach. He gave a laugh and shook his head slowly. How different a trip from the beach will be compared to traversing the length of the desert to get to it. The universe has been kind indeed.

Cory fell asleep but woke as the night grew chilly. He stumbled his way to the little hut and the pile of bedding he'd seen earlier. He felt his body and mind relax and slept soundly until early light when he started to dress and gather his things. It was then that it finally and truly dawned on him that he need not take everything with him. I can come back. What I need will be here waiting for me to return. I can come here any time I want, just like I can go to the hills or to the Japanese bridge. The desert is a part of me just as this ocean is. I can discard what I no longer need and know it will be replaced with what I need now.

CHAPTER 6

Cory pulled the pouch out of the larger bag and made a small packet of food. After checking that his water bottle was full and that the conch shell was still in his pocket, he started out. He wondered if Zanzibar would come with him. He knew the way and why he was going, so it didn't matter, but he'd like her company. He walked on the firm sand by the water's edge. The colors in the east extended tentative fingers into the western sky, and waves lapped softly near his feet.

Halfway to his destination, he stopped to eat. As he sat on the sand and watched sun and clouds play over the desert, uncomfortable thoughts about the cave started to sneak in. They made themselves comfortable and soon crowded his mind. He muttered, "Luke Skywalker," and started feeling anxious.

What things might his own cave experience dredge up? The peace of the previous evening and early morning started to run like wet paint in the rain. Cory could all but see the colors disappear into an indistinguishable mass. This was no way to start. He tried to tame his thoughts, get the individual colors back. Caves teach us, he reminded himself. They are a womb, an incubation. Being born is uncomfortable and messy but so very worth all the pain. His thoughts slowly realigned, the colors organizing themselves back into a picture. Not a picture that was altogether clear yet, but something much better than the muddy mess they had been.

Cory got up and brushed crumbs and sand from his jeans. He said aloud, "Thank you for the desert and the ocean, for a coyote and a bee, and for the cave that's coming." With that, he turned inland away from the packed sand to the pebbles and slipping sand of the desert. It took less than an hour to reach the cave. Cory's calves were aching from constantly needing to adjust his steps. There were fewer pebbles than on yesterday's more northern route, and the sand slid, making him grasp with his feet. The rise, though long and low, was not the stroll the beach had been earlier. It's good practice for what's coming, he reminded himself.

Before he was ready, Cory found himself standing at the cave's entrance. He was about to enter when he heard a hawk's cry. He stepped back to search the sky. No hawk, just the echo of its voice, but he did see a small mass of fuzzy darkness coming towards him. All birds look dark against the sky, he reminded himself. Still, he was torn: take shelter in the cave or wait to see what was coming. He did not feel he was supposed to enter the cave yet, but maybe the growing mass in the sky was a sign that he should. Before his thinking could become confused, he remembered to look within himself to find his ocean. Anxiety washed out of him to be replaced with hope and resolve, only a quiet ripple, but enough.

He shaded his eyes and looked again. Laughing aloud, he stretched out his arms. Dozens of bees began to land on him. Cory soon became aware that not all bees are the same. Some landed gently like Zanzibar and the ones yesterday. Others plopped. It was a funny sensation. They also tickled, and Cory was trying not to laugh. He wasn't sure what they'd make of it if he started shaking, but he couldn't help it. They didn't seem to mind. In fact, they seemed to join in with him. They walked around on him as if he belonged to them, mostly on his clothing and arms but a few on his face. Abruptly, they became still.

Cory looked at his thumb. "Hi, Zanzibar. I'm really glad you came and brought the hive."

Cory walked slowly to the cave entrance and stepped inside. He didn't have to go far until the passage gave way to a space big enough to make a cozy home for a small family. It was all rock and seemingly empty, no feeling of something hidden. Cory found a low ledge, sat and rested his hands on his legs. The bees on his arms and jeans quietly repositioned themselves. They all waited. Nothing happened. Nothing seemed to want or need to happen. "Zanzibar?"

She hovered in front of him eye-to-eye much like adults do when they want to make very sure the child in front of them will understand what they're about to say. "I'm listening." *Not good enough.* Cory thought for a moment. "Okay, I'm listening, I will hear, and I will accept what you tell me no matter what it is." Zanzibar bobbed a bit. Well, that's new, thought Cory. Then, he smiled and thought, no; that's how we met, Zanzibar-the-magic-wand bobbing as a shadow in the desert, asking me to follow and believe. And I did and so glad that I did. "Please, what's your message?" he asked preparing himself to accept that evil was his father or worse, that his fiancée had been correct ... he was nothing.

He breathed out and looked at Zanzibar. She hovered quietly. *There's nothing here like you're expecting. You took care of it all out there. You don't need a cave experience, at least right now. You are welcome to come to the cave when you want. It will always be here to welcome you, to give you its gifts and take from you what needs to be left behind, but you needn't test yourself today.*

Cory sat stunned. It didn't seem as if he'd given enough, that this birth had been painful enough, or that he had, what ... suffered enough? Then he asked himself, why should learning be about suffering? He held the pouch but did not take the objects out as he carefully reviewed his life. Most of his learning, like the desert experience yesterday, was a mixture of easy and difficult, pleasant and sad, joyful and scary. Only the one had been heart wrenching, but even it had had moments of great happiness. He looked up. *Yes,* answered Zanzibar.

There is one thing here for you. "Yes?" asked Cory eagerly. *Look down.* Waiting at his feet for him to notice it was a small blue and green agate shot through with white. The whole journey in an agate. He picked it up and placed it carefully in the pouch. His whole life in an agate. He found he was crying. The bees lifted off to let him cry as he wanted. The cave accepted his tears and dried them for him.

After a bit, Cory walked out, a train of bees accompanying him. As they made their way back to the cabana, Cory said to Zanzibar, "The trip is so long. I can't imagine I can get here often. Is this why cave experiences are rather rare?" *Not at all,* she replied. *They're as close as they need to be.* Cory didn't understand, but he let it go. They walked—well, he walked and she rode—companionably back to the cabana and ocean.

CHAPTER 7

Cory ate lunch and rested his eyes, body, and mind in the pull and flow of the tide. He wished again he could paint it. The idea sidled up nearer to him. Maybe he could get someone to paint it for him. Of course, that would mean letting another person into his zoo and giving up control of where that person went or what that person might do. The idea sat down next to him and prepared to make itself comfortable. It would also mean any painting would be that person's vision and not his, but maybe it would be okay. What would be okay? he asked himself. Okay to let another person onto the estate? Okay to let another person have a different vision? "It didn't work out so well the last time," he reminded himself. But the idea asked him to take that chance again. *Please take the chance*, it whispered into his ear *because it's already on its way to you.*

Cory stretched his neck and shoulders and then sighed. After everything that's happened in the last day ... after everything that's happened in my whole life! He shook his head. There's only one answer. "Yes." Too quickly to be ready for her, Daisy fluttered onto his knee. He put a finger out and she climbed on. "Dais. Where did you come from?" *Along the beach.* "I didn't pass you. I would have seen you." *No, from the other direction. I brought you someone.* "I didn't know I wanted someone." *I did.*

Cory looked south where he had not yet explored. As he started towards the clump of palms visible where the coastline turned east, he saw a person emerge. He was startled and ready to be upset that Daisy had let someone in, but he had known for years that Daisy would never hurt him, not by intention or even by accident. Everything she had done for him throughout the years had been to help him. He relaxed and walked towards his visitor.

The woman looked up and stopped when she saw Cory. When he reached her, she apologized, "I came because ... well, I followed a little bird. It seemed the thing to do. I hope it's okay. I assume this is all yours?"

"It is," said Cory. All he could do was to stare at her. He tore his gaze away, knowing it was rude and probably making her think he was weird. "I'm Cory. I'm a zoo keeper and a guide." He'd never added that. Is that who he was now?

He pulled himself away from his reeling thoughts to what she was saying, "I'm Ellie. I'm a, I'm an artist." Cory wanted to laugh and cry and jump up and down and run around and hug her. He refrained from all of it and said calmly, "Welcome. I'd like to show you something." As it was just late afternoon, they still had several hours to wait. Cory spent them asking Ellie about herself and telling her about his zoo. The phrase "you had me at" came to mind when she said she didn't like to see animals caged. "Me either," said Cory. "None of mine are. They are free to come and go."

"I think I like your zoo," said Ellie shyly, and Cory hoped she meant she liked him, too, because he thought he might grow to like her a lot. She had pulled out a pad of thick paper and some colored pencils and had been sketching as they talked. She now showed him her picture.

Cory blinked and said reverently, "That's how I see it, too." It was a simple picture of the surf, but Cory could see through the colors of the water to the mountains and valleys beneath. He pulled the little conch shell out of his pocket. "I think this is meant for you," and handed it to her. "I found it yesterday," and told her the story of the desert, of Ralph and Zanzibar and the hawk. When he was finished, he looked to see how she might have taken it all.

She was looking at him as if it was the most common thing in the world to follow a coyote and a bee through the desert to an ocean. "Do you know that Ralph means wolf counsel and one of the things wolves symbolize is understanding?"

"No, I didn't," said Cory. "It fits though."

"Yes, it does." She smiled at him. "Thank you for the shell. It's lovely."

"You're welcome." He thought a moment and asked, "Do you know what Zanzibar means?"

"No. It might not mean anything like 'strong' or 'majestic'. It may just be a place name."

"That could work, too," said Cory as he thought, I think I'm finding my new place. "Are you real?" he asked suddenly.

Ellie's laugh was like rain on a water chain, soft and silvery. "I'm very real," she said, "Are you?"

"Oh, very much so." Cory brought food from the cabana, and they ate and watched the ocean. Ellie sketched. Cory thought. He broke the quiet with, "I wasn't thinking about practicalities. I wanted you to see my ocean at dusk, but the hut isn't a proper place to spend the night. Should we go?"

Ellie looked up confused, "I thought the house I passed on the way in was yours, too."

Cory's turn to be confused, he asked, "When did you pass a house? A white house with dark green shutters and a blue door?"

She nodded. "This afternoon, not fifteen minutes from where I met you. I don't understand." She asked gently, "You don't know where your house is?" wondering if he had gotten sun stroke.

Cory thought how to give the answer. She probably thought he was deranged. "I've never traveled this way before. Until yesterday afternoon, I didn't even know I had an ocean. My home is really that close?"

Ellie smiled, relieved, and nodded. "I understand now. Sometimes what is so obvious to others is completely hidden from ourselves. Can we stay and see dusk?"

"Absolutely," replied Cory. They sat and watched the colors start to change. Daisy flew in and landed on Ellie's sketchpad. "Daisychain," said Cory looking fondly at her. She cocked her head. *What?* "Just Daisychain."

"Is that like saying, "Eleanor Margaret or Ellie May-y?"

"Definitely Ellie May-y." said Cory. "Dais likes to surprise me. Sometimes I think she gets a bit ahead of me though." Daisy looked at him. *You're ready. You just keep putting off thinking about it, but it's time.*

"I've been calling her Gertrude," said Ellie, "Trudy for short. Her name is Daisychain?"

"Daisy and Dais for short, but sometimes I call her Daisychain as a special nickname," said Cory fondly stroking Daisy's downy breast feathers as she preened and then flew off on a Daisy mission. It then occurred to him to ask, "How long have you known Daisy, Gertrude?"

"Oh, only a few days, no, maybe a week or two," said Ellie thinking back. "She met me on the sidewalk one day and went sketching with me. I hadn't sketched in so long. She just kind of kept showing up."

"Yes, she does," and Cory told her his and Daisy's story.

"I wonder how many others she's guided," considered Ellie. "I'll bet there are quite a few."

Cory sat stunned. He knew Daisy was special but that she had guided others, that he was part of a group, maybe a group that existed over time and space.? He was part of a community? "I wonder if the others have extraordinary experiences like I do." He turned to Ellie, "and like I assume you've had." She nodded slowly and smiled into Cory's eyes.

"The sky and waves are incredible," offered Ellie.

Cory had completely forgotten about them and turned to look. She was right. The sunset gilded the surface as with vermeil: silver under the surface and golds and pinks on top. They waited until the colors started to fade and then followed their earlier path back to the palms where they turned inland. Cory could see his roof as they made the turn. Not to know it was there. Not to know he had an ocean so close. At his front door, he invited Ellie in.

"I should get home," she said shyly. "and it's not far."

"I'll walk you there," said Cory.

"Sure you can find your way back?" she teased.

"Yes. I can now," said Cory. She smiled and led the way to her house. She was right. It was only about twenty minutes away. "Would you like a tour of another part of the estate tomorrow?"

"Oh, very much."

"I could pick you up at 10:00. Is that too early?"

"Oh no, I'm an early riser."

"In that case, how about a morning tour and breakfast. I make a great paella."

"Okay, but you don't need to fetch me. I can find my way. How early, 8:00?"

"That's perfect. I'm glad you followed Daisy, Gertrude."

"Me too. Good night, Cory." She said it gently as if it might soon be said fondly.

"Good night, Ellie."

Cory walked home in a daze of happiness. He, at least, had a new friend, and maybe she'd turn into something more. He shouldn't be this happy. He needed to be more cautious. It felt so right. But seven years ago, he thought he'd been right. But he'd been so young then. He knew so much more now.

He walked to the Japanese bridge, his longtime go-to place for thinking. No one joined him. That was okay. He didn't think he could absorb more lessons right now. He stood still and let the estate's peace soothe him and reviewed his experiences of the last two days.

Daisy flapped in. She seemed tired. Cory scooped her up and made a nest of his hands. "We need to talk, Daisy Gertrude." She looked at him seemingly waiting. Cory reflected, shook his head, and looked at her fondly and a bit in awe. "What have you been up to, Daisychain?" *My job.* Cory just shook his head and looked over the water and let his mind slide to the ocean as he held Daisy in the nest of his hands. It was as if he could see his future, a rich and bright one, rolling out in front of him, and it seemed to include a new friend and his new job. He had no more energy right now to think about anything. Daisy was asleep in his hands, and he carried her carefully home.

CHAPTER 8

The next morning, Cory got up extra early and went to the bridge to think before starting to prepare for his visitor. The sun was barely emerging above the bamboo fronds, and the air was moist and still cool. This was his favorite time of day. "Good morning," he said quietly to everyone and everything. The breeze and bamboo responded. Several ducks paddled in the rushes. A bird started twittering in a tree, then another. A fish jumped in the water and made a small ripple that sparkled as it fanned out over the lake.

What does it mean for me now to be a guide? Cory wondered. I still need guiding myself.

The breeze whispered, *I go where I'm sent. I don't know where that will be until I'm almost there. There'd be no breeze if I waited to know. I need guiding, too.*

So do I, rustled the bamboo. *I grow because it's written within me. I don't know how to do it. I just do it because it needs to be done.*

I guess I just trust and walk and trust some more, thought Cory. "And walk some more," he said as he headed back to the house to put the paella in the oven.

He was setting the little table in the kitchen when he heard a knock. "Good morning," he said as he held the door open. He noticed Ellie had a large, straw hat with her and was wearing a long, unbleached-cotton dress with crocheted edges. She looked like she should be in a century-old painting, and he wondered again if she was real. She wore her long, dark hair loose. She looked fresh and ... Cory searched for the word. Unpretentious. Real. He smiled.

He has such a beautiful smile, thought Ellie. It's so warm and open. "Good morning," she said smiling back.

"I'm glad you accepted my invitation." He led the way to the kitchen. "When I asked, I wasn't sure you would."

"Two days ago, I'm not sure I would have either, but Gertrude, Daisy convinced me."

"Of course, she did. She's a determined little chickadee."

"She certainly is. I've always known about helper animals, totem animals, but I never had one. I've wanted one. When she first showed up, I wasn't sure who she was, but I found myself wanting to sketch again. Until a few days ago, I hadn't been out to sketch in a long, long time. And when she showed up yesterday, she kept fluttering near me and directing my steps towards your zoo. So, I finally gave up and just followed her. And that seemed to work out well. Last evening, she came by wanting to tell me about you. She told me I can trust you."

Cory turned away towards the stove to hide the smile that had taken over his face. Feeling he needed to say something, he offered, "I think she needs a new name. We can't keep calling her Gertrude Trudy Daisy Dais Daisychain."

"No, I guess not," laughed Ellie. "Any ideas?" Cory thought, then shook his head. "Let's see. How about ... " Ellie went through Rachel, Robin, Rochelle. Stuck at R, she started again. Victoria, Tamara, Dulcie ... and finally said, "How about Constance?"

"I like that a lot," said Cory, "And she certainly is constant."

"It means strong willed." Ellie pulled out her phone. A moment later, she added, "and hero."

"Of course, it does. We'll tell her when she shows up. I think she'll like it. How do you know so much about the meanings of names?"

"Oh, it came along with my art. When I paint, I incorporate objects, plants, rocks, just anything that has a meaningful name that fits what I'm seeing. I guess you'd call it symbolic art or something."

"I'm hoping you'll want to paint what you see on the estate. Recently, I've found myself wishing I could paint what I see, but I'm no painter. And, I like what you said about names. I can tell you the animals' names, but I named them what they seemed like to me. I didn't think about what their names might mean. I can tell you most of the plants' names, too." Cory laughed, "I don't mean like Hank or Stephanie or even their genus and species. I mean like acacia and rhododendron."

"Oh, plants have their own meanings. Everything has meaning." Cory put breakfast on the table. "It all looks and smells so good. Thank you, Cory."

After breakfast, Cory gathered Ellie's portfolio and a picnic basket and handed her a blanket to carry. "I thought we could go to the hills. They are really lovely in summer," he said. "But first ... " he whistled for Daisy. When they saw her coming, Ellie put out her hand.

"Daisy dear," she said. "I've been calling you Trudy and learned only yesterday your name is Daisy." *I have lots of names.*

Cory stepped next to Ellie. "We thought we'd give you a new name from both of us." Daisy hopped around looking at them. "Do you like Constance? Connie for short?" They waited. "I've never seen you be shy before," remarked Cory. "We'll still call you by the pet names we have for you, Dais."

"What do you think, Trudy?" coaxed Ellie. Daisy got quiet and settled in. "I think she likes it all," said Ellie.

They walked, Constance Gertrude Daisy flew, to the nearest hills. A number of them had trees, but many were meadows of wildflowers. They sat on a large rock and surveyed a valley of irises.

"I've never seen so many colors of irises," said Ellie in awe. "Never. You are quite some person, Cory."

"I am?"

"Oh, yes. They're yours, right?"

"Yes," he admitted.

"Well, irises represent the rainbow, and the rainbow and its colors are rich, rich, rich with meaning. So, you are quite something." Connie was hopping about behind Ellie's back. *Told you so told you so.* She was clearly delighted.

"Wow," said Cory. "Thank you for thinking I'm something."

"Well, you are," laughed Ellie softly. "You're Cory, a guide and keeper of a special zoo, and you are very kind. Connie wouldn't have stayed with you if you weren't."

It occurred to Cory to ask, "Ellie? Why did you accept my invitation yesterday to see the ocean? It occurs to me now that it was an odd invitation from a total stranger. I'm curious."

"Oh," said Ellie, "Well, you see, I, uh ... "

"I didn't mean to pry," Cory interrupted apologetically. "I feel I've known you forever instead of less than a day; well, and that was rude to ask, wasn't it? I'm sorry."

"No, no, it's okay. I shouldn't be embarrassed. I don't have anything to be embarrassed about," said Ellie straightening her shoulders and tossing her hair back. "It was the way you treated me. I felt I could trust you, and that hasn't happened in a long time." She paused, sighed, and finally continued, "You see, I've drawn and painted since I was little. It's all I ever wanted to do. I got accepted at a top-notch art school and graduated with honors. I had several shows and sold some pieces. Everyone thought I was going to go big. I thought I might go fairly big, not be shown in New York galleries or major museums like the Met but certainly in respectable ones that more than a few people have heard of. I had it all planned." Her voice trailed off. She looked up and smiled wanly at Cory.

He hated putting her through this. It felt like it was his fault because he'd asked. He looked away not able to bear her pain and saw Connie sitting quietly on a nearby rock. He took comfort and strength from her and took Ellie's hand. She blinked and looked at him.

"Ever had your dreams so thoroughly dashed you aren't sure you can get up again?" He nodded. "I finally got my break and was introduced to THE man, the big mover and shaker, who would make my career, except instead, he said he didn't know how I'd gotten into art school. He said he wouldn't have let me into even a mediocre one. The people who told me I had talent were idiots and should be fired if they were professors and have their canvases slashed if they were working artists. He said my vision was insipid and hackneyed."

"He said much worse. He eviscerated not just my art but me. After he got done, which included spreading his opinion to everyone he could, no one would touch me. My career was over, and it hadn't even started. It felt like my life was over. Invitations to show were canceled, invitations to parties were nonexistent."

They were quiet a moment, and then Ellie went on, "I found out who my friends were. Not many stayed. I hadn't picked well, but it didn't matter. I didn't want to see anyone anyway. I didn't do much for a long time. But, finally, I had to go to work, so I got a job at the college library. I didn't have to talk to people, just reshelve books and catalogue. It was almost more than I could handle for the first few months. I read a lot." She sighed.

"A couple of months ago, a few girlfriends got me go to lunch with them. One recommended a book she had just finished and enjoyed. It had an artist in it. That helped enough that I decided I didn't have to give up art for myself. Maybe nobody else wanted to see it, but I wanted to produce it. I drew some at home. It felt so good to draw again and to feel my hands making what my mind saw. So, I decided to go out and sketch. If people saw me and saw my pictures and thought they were nothing, well, it didn't matter. But when you treated me like someone who could appreciate what you have and like an artist; well, how could I refuse?"

Cory was seething but remembered that the man needed love and Light as much as anyone else, maybe more. He made a quick prayer for him, whoever he was, and then asked, "How long ... ?" Cory's voice broke and he cleared his throat. "How long ago did that terrible man do that?"

"About, oh, maybe two years ago, not quite."

"It's awful. No one's dreams should be obliterated like that. I just want to cry."

"It's okay now, I think. You know, it wasn't just that he said those things. It was that, all of a sudden, everyone else acted like they believed him. They chimed in. After a while, it wears you down, and you start believing it, too." She looked at him. "I can't imagine it's been easy being keeper of an estate for helper animals."

Cory thought about that. "I parted ways with some so-called friends, but, on the whole, I've been extremely fortunate in my life to have people who understand me, or if they don't quite understand, at least accept me. I learned a lesson kind of like yours about seven years ago and have chosen people more carefully since. The animals are easy," he added suddenly smiling. A chipmunk had boldly approached and was sitting in some flowers just below Ellie.

"What's his name?" Ellie asked.

"I don't have a chipmunk." Cory answered, smiling a small secret smile.

"You do now."

"Nope; he's yours."

Ellie looked at Cory in amazement. He nodded and smiled. "Really? Oh, that's, oh! Should I name him?"

"If you want to."

"Is your zoo always this magical?"

"Most days." He looked around; how lucky I am, he thought, and then added, Thank You, as he looked up to the sky and beyond.

"I hope she'll, I think she's a she, hope she'll sit still so I can sketch her." Cory remained quiet while Ellie slowly opened her pad and sketched what she saw. When she was finished, she said, "Thank you, Cora. You were an excellent model."

After Cora scampered off, Cory said, "Cora, huh?" and moved over to see the picture.

"Yes, Cora," came Ellie's definite reply. It was just a soft-pencil drawing, shading mostly, but Cora sat front and center in the midst of flowers and grasses, ants and field mice, butterflies and breezes, an ocean beneath and eternity above.

Cory shook his head. He could see the universe in a few lines of pencil on paper. "That man was wrong, so wrong," he said surveying what she'd drawn, trying to enter it, really.

"I like to think so," said Ellie critically eyeing the drawing.

"I think you should show yesterday's and this one to someone."

"No, not yet," said Ellie abruptly closing the sketch pad.

"I may not know what names mean," Cory began tentatively, "but I know a chipmunk showing up means to live a little."

"It does?" Ellie asked turning to him. Cory nodded. "I'll consider it then," she replied softly.

"That's a start. In the meantime, how about walking over to the lake to look for ducklings?"

"You have ducklings?" she asked, enchanted.

"Yup. You ready?" Cory offered her his hand to help her up and kept it as they strolled towards the lake.

CHAPTER 9

Over the remaining summer, Cory and Ellie spent most of their time on the estate learning about each other's crafts and about each other. By the time fall came, Ellie was ready to show her art to someone other than Cory. She now had quite a few sketches and paintings of animals, landscapes, Cory's favorite thinking spot on the crest of the Japanese bridge, his front porch, and, of course, many of Connie or of Connie and Cora. She decided to present the first two sketches to a gallery owner one of Cory's friends knew. Cory said he would take them in. They were as yet unsigned.

"Don't you want to put your name on them?" Cory asked as Ellie packed them in a portfolio.

"I can't yet. It feels like an invitation for the world to mock me. If he hates them, I can keep them for myself. I know they're mine without a signature."

"All right," Cory relented.

Ellie waited anxiously at a nearby café. The day was bright, the sun warm, and a cool breeze wafted in. Tiny butterflies flitted through the potted plants adorning the outside seating area where Ellie waited. A bee buzzed through and inspected her coffee before leaving for sweeter offerings.

After what seemed much longer than it was, Ellie saw Cory and a man she didn't know walking quickly towards her. Cory was beaming. She thought he might start dancing. The man pulled ahead of Cory and as he reached her, Ellie stood.

He extended his hands and took her offered hand in both of his. "Your sketches are marvelous, wonderful, so full of life and, and the things we can't see but know in our souls are there. They are, they are simply wondrous," he repeated. On the way to meet her, he'd rehearsed a whole speech that now failed him.

"Thank you," said Ellie, greatly surprised. Cory couldn't quit beaming.

They ordered drinks and got down to business. "I've heard of you, of course," the man said. As Ellie blushed, he shook his head and said, "I never believed him. I'd seen some of your student work. It was a shame. A total shame. I so hoped you'd surface again at some point." He thought, hesitated and then added, "The beauty you create," he smiled gently at her, "the beauty you are is a magnet for some to try to wound, to destroy, even. It scares them."

"Scares them?" Ellie asked perplexed.

"They can't find themselves in it, and since they think they are everything, they have to tear it down to something in which they can see themselves. It's always been this way." He stopped then started again. "I'm sorry I didn't have the reputation to be able to defend you then."

"He would have hurt you, too." Ellie hoped that didn't sound rude. She had recognized Michel de Sant's name when he introduced himself. He had been a big name then but not big enough. He was a much bigger name now. She had no idea that was who Cory was taking her sketches to. He'd said a friend of a friend and didn't say more.

"He can't now or you either. If you'll let me, I want everything you have drawn and painted in the last few months. I'd like to include you in what was going to be a three-person show. I'd like it to be a four-person show."

"I don't know," Ellie began, looking to Cory. "This has to be Cory's decision, too. It's his estate." Right on cue, the bee came back and landed on the table, walked around, and then flitted off again.

Ellie looked at Cory. "That's her," he said, "and you know I'd love others to see the estate as you do."

"Then, yes," said Ellie, "I'll do it."

Michel de Sant followed them back to the estate and took Ellie's pictures away with him. "I feel bereft," she said and wandered aimlessly until Cora came to distract her.

The next few weeks were a flurry of activity: appointments at the studio, coaching from Michel's assistant about pricing, commissions, and how to handle invitations from other gallery owners. Ellie was already exhausted, and she still needed a dress for the opening. She asked her friend Jeana to go with her.

Cory liked Jeana and her boyfriend, Derek. It was nice to have a couple to go to dinner with, and they were in awe of the estate and the animals. Ellie liked Jeana but found her a bit tiring. As she was getting ready to leave, she said, "Jeana's a bit bossy, but she has a good eye for clothes. Something I don't have."

"What do you mean?" Cory asked. "I think you have a lot of style just the way you are."

"I'll keep that in mind as she tries to get me to do my nails and change my hair and put on heels." Cory looked appalled as they heard a car horn honk.

He hugged her and whispered, "Don't let Jeana talk you into anything that's not you." She kissed him on the cheek and said, "Don't worry."

But now he was. He couldn't help it. He didn't want to lose the wonderful little parts of her he was discovering. He knew he wouldn't lose her out of his life, but he wanted to keep her quirkiness. Hearing a hawk, he looked up, laughed to himself, and said, "You're right. I just need to trust."

Connie flew in. *What's up?* "Hey, Connie. I was being my lesser self." She looked as shocked as a chickadee can. "I know. I started thinking outside the estate and lost my focus." *Yes, we sensed that was happening.* "Who's we?" *Berkeley and me.* It dawned on Cory. "That's the hawk's name? You two longtime friends?" *Yes and yes.* "Well, thank you both for showing up. Ellie is out shopping with a friend who wants to turn her into I don't know what." *Oh, no worries.* "Really?" *Yes, let's enjoy the afternoon. Let's go to the gazebo.* "Okay. I haven't been there in a long time." Cory strolled leisurely over the bridge and took the path that cut through a field of daisies. "Now I know why you wanted to come this way, Daisychain," he teased.

Cory lowered himself into one of the wicker chairs. It was peaceful here, and soon he felt calmer and clearer. While Cory looked and thought, daydreamed and napped, Connie flitted through the field and bounced on flower stems.

CHAPTER 10

Ellie wasn't having as successful a mission as she had hoped. Jeana, as usual, was bossing, with little success, but it was wearing Ellie out. "I'm me. If you think I should cut my hair in some artsy way, why can't I just wear what I like and be natural, artsy me?" Ellie complained as Jeana dragged her from store to store. She finally decided she had had enough of Jeana's brow beating and was rehearsing how she could say this to her. When they stopped to cross yet another street to the next row of retailers, Ellie looked down the side street and spotted a sign that had *Louise's Finery* written in fancy script. Underneath, it read *The Look You're Looking For.* "Let's see what's down here," said Ellie.

"Oh, those are boutiques, way too expensive. The next block will have something." The walk light came on, Jeana was about to cross, but Ellie had already started down the side street. "Ellie, really!"

"I want to look in this shop," said Ellie with more confidence.

"I thought you asked me to come along because you don't know what you're doing, and I do," Jeana said in disgust. "You've turned down so many appropriate dresses. Really nice ones."

Ellie stopped. "But they aren't me, Jeana. I wanted you to come because it would be fun to have you along, and you know clothes, and I value your opinion. But the choice has to be mine." She thought a moment and added, "No one will blame you if I end up looking ridiculous in what I choose. I won't say, 'Oh, I unfortunately let Jeana talk me into this. Such a mistake.'" She added, "tut, tut" with her tongue and had a roguish look she hoped would lighten the mood. A chipmunk eating nasturtiums in a nearby planter munched and looked on. It closed its eyes a moment and then disappeared into the shadows of the leaves.

Not used to being challenged, Jeana still looked put out but followed her into the shop. Turning to Ellie, she said, "All right. Let's see what you can do. I'm going to sit over here." She made herself at home in a plush chair and pulled out her phone.

*   *   *

After a long rest, Cory roused himself. Connie was napping on his leg. She woke up when he shifted his weight. "I haven't been to the hive in a while." He looked at her, "Want to come along?" *No, you go. I have some other things to do.*

Cory stepped out from under the gazebo. As he passed the house, he admired the planters and tiled tables Ellie had added to the porch. He took the cobblestone path to the very back of the yard where he and Ellie had planted protective trees and bushes and flowers that bees like. When he showed it to Zanzibar, she had moved the hive, as Cory called the bees, from the desert to the new bee garden.

The bees were bumbling from flower to flower, flower to hive and back again. Cory approached slowly until he saw they knew it was him, and then he stopped and put out his arms. They flew in, landing softly or in plops until he was covered. He felt them get still and looked at his right thumb and smiled. "Hi Zanzibar. Everything okay? You and the hive need anything?" *We're good. You provided well for us.* "You've provided so very well for me. Send someone if you need anything. I'll check back in a few days." With that, they all lifted off except for Zanzibar. "I'm hoping Ellie and Jeana are back." *I'll come with you.* "I'd love to have your company." She settled on Cory's thumb, which he kept out front a bit by resting his elbow against his side.

Ellie and Jeana were getting out of the car as Cory came around the house. He saw that Ellie had a long dress bag with her and looked excited. As Cory walked up, Jeana's eyes got big and she stepped back. She pointed to his thumb and whispered, "You have a bee on you, don't move."

"This is Zanzibar. We wanted to see how the shopping trip went."

"Oh, Cory, wait 'til you see it. It's gorgeous." Ellie was sparkling.

Cory looked at Jeana. "Don't look at me. Ellie found it. I didn't even want to go in that shop."

"But when you saw it, you screamed, 'That's the one,' and scared the other customers," giggled Ellie. They both burst out laughing.

"I want to see it, too," said Cory.

Ellie started to get it out of the bag when Cory said, "No, on you."

"Go put it on, honey. We'll wait here for you," ordered Jeana, but she did it more congenially than Cory had heard her before. Ellie took her bags and headed for the house.

Jeana then surprised Cory by asking, "May I hold your bee?"

"If she'll let you; it's her choice," said Cory. "Hold your finger out." Jeana did so and Zanzibar made an arc from Cory's thumb to Jeana's finger.

"She tickles," said Jeana, but she calmed herself and lifted her finger so that she and Zanzibar were at eye level. "She's really marvelous, isn't she?"

"Yes," agreed Cory simply.

"How do you know her name is Zanzibar? For that matter, how do you know she's a she?"

"I named her," said Cory, "and I know she's a she because she's the queen of the hive."

Zanzibar flew off. "I wish I had a bee or any animal," said Jeana wistfully.

"I imagine you have one," said Cory. "Animals adopt us to teach us, to help us work on areas in our lives where we need help."

"How can I find my animal?" asked Jeana.

"It finds you. Watch for animals that show up in your life when and where you least expect them."

"I saw a raccoon in the backyard the other afternoon."

"He or she may be yours then. Raccoons are not often found in town during the day. It wasn't acting weird, was it?"

"No. It sauntered through from the hedge, across the grass to the trees at the back. I only saw it because I was folding laundry in the breakfast room."

They heard the screen door close. Cory almost cried when he saw Ellie. She looked like a princess. The dress was gauzy with many layers and colors that blended one into the other. The irregular hem ended mid-calf. She was wearing simple but elegant sandals and had gathered her hair into a chignon.

"See why I screamed?" asked Jeana.

"I certainly do," replied Cory unable to tear his gaze from Ellie.

"Well? What do you think?" asked Ellie.

"You look magical, like a fairy princess," said Cory walking up to her.

"Aww, thank you, honey. Jeana suggested the sandals and hairstyle. I think they're perfect."

"You look elegant, refined, and artsy," pronounced Cory.

"Then I guess I have it all covered. I'm going to go change. I don't want anything happening to the dress. It's too close to the show to have to find a different one."

CHAPTER 11

The evening before the show, Ellie and Cory went to see how everything was laid out. Michel had told her she could bring three people. So, Jeana and Derek came along for moral support. Next to the gallery's name on the marquee was a banner that read *Our Futures, Our Pasts*.

"Wow, Ellie," said Derek stopping on the sidewalk to read it. "That's really cool."

"Thank you," Ellie said faintly as she smiled at them. When she turned to Cory, he could see she was beginning to realize she was about to show her art to other people. He put his arm around her.

"It's going to be okay. It is okay," He whispered and gave her a quick squeeze. She nodded uncertainly.

Michel's assistant met them at the door and let them in. "Welcome. Mr. de Sant will be out in a moment. Two of the other artists are here already. Please make yourselves at home and look around. Each of you has your own area. Ellie, your pieces are over here." They said their thanks and tried to take it all in before venturing any direction. The large gallery was effectively divided into five areas by movable walls. The front area had been set up with linen-draped tables for food and drinks. Each artist had an area carefully lighted and arranged to show their pieces to best advantage.

Just with a cursory glance, Ellie could see no one's space was better positioned than any of the others. She could also see how different all their works were. A piece or two invited from each area and drew the viewer in to see more. Cory, Jeana, and Derek went straight to Ellie's area. Ellie wandered over to a multimedia installation. The artist was standing there looking dumfounded. "Hi, I'm Ellie Sanborn. First show?" she asked.

He nodded. "Jason Levine, and, yes."

"Mine, too, really." She looked around his area. "I like how you incorporated the textiles into the natural elements."

Jason spent a few minutes explaining his concepts and vision to her and then asked, "Where are your pieces?"

"Over here."

Cory, Jeana, and Derek had moved on to see the other artists' works. Jason made several slow circles around Ellie's space. Michel had grouped her sketches and paintings by area of the estate. All pictures that included the Japanese bridge and lake were grouped together. Paintings of the hills full of summer flowers covered another wall. But sketches and small watercolors Ellie had done of Connie were placed throughout the display. A small oil of Cora sitting in a field of flowers and holding a daisy was placed so it was the last piece people would see on their way out. "This is your signature, your brand," Michel had told Ellie when he found it in her studio the day he had taken her pieces to the gallery. "This one you will not sell."

"Is this place real?" Jason asked. Ellie nodded smiling. "Where is it?"

Ellie pulled out one of their cards and handed it to him. "You're welcome any time, Jason. Just call us a day or so ahead of when you'd like to visit." Hearing Ellie's invitation, Cory came back. "Cory, this is Jason Levine. He has the multimedia over there. I've invited him to come out to the estate."

The men shook hands, and Cory remarked, "I really like that big piece with the driftwood in it. I want to come over and have you tell me about your other works." The three chatted for a few minutes before Jason excused himself. After he left, Cory asked, "You usually don't spontaneously invite people to the estate. You have something in mind, don't you?"

"Jason has a sweet spirit about him, and he seems to need a community. I thought he might like ours."

"You are so wonderful," said Cory putting his arm protectively and lovingly around her as he gently kissed her hair. The fourth artist arrived, Michel came out, and they got down to pre-show business.

The next evening, Ellie and Cory arrived early. Ellie had wanted to bring Cora for moral support, but Cory talked her out of it. "It's going to be awfully crowded and probably noisy. I don't think she'll like it."

"Yes, I'm sure that's true," Ellie replied.

Cory could tell she was nervous. "Honey, don't worry. Your natural charm will win everyone over. Besides, you don't have a pocket big enough for her to ride in."

"You're right," agreed Ellie. At one seam, her dress had a small, secret pocket that was big enough to put a folded bill and maybe a tissue, but Cora certainly couldn't fit. They were on their way to the car when Ellie brightened suddenly. "I'll be right back." Cory waited by the car. Ellie hurried into the bedroom and sorted through her jewelry box and came back seemingly with nothing. When she reached the car, she opened her hand to show Cory the tiny conch shell he had given her the day they met. "This is perfect," she said happily and dropped it into the pocket.

When they got to the gallery, Cory put his hands on her shoulders and said, "I'll be available, but I don't want to crowd you."

"Okay," she nodded, smiling, but she still looked anxious.

Michel stopped by each artist's area to give last minute coaching and advice, "Just breathe. Breathe and enjoy."

Everyone's excitement was palpable. Ellie was still trying to get her pulse to quit pounding in her ears when the first visitor entered. More people arrived. Several wandered into her area. Ellie smiled and made herself greet them. Cory caught her eye and winked at her, which helped. She felt her heart quit thudding quite as loudly. Soon, people began gathering around her paintings. After the first person asked her a question, Ellie began overcoming her nervousness. She realized talking to them about her art was easy. They were interested and viewed her as the expert she was.

Not long into the evening, Ellie felt simultaneously drained and exhilarated. For the most part, people were complimentary. She heard words such as "mystical," "spiritual," and "visionary" as they discussed her work. Collectors gave her their cards as did critics and gallery owners. They all took her cards in return. No one who knew about Ellie's past mentioned it to her, but once they realized who Cory was, several were bold enough to tell him they were glad she had found her voice again. By the end of the evening, half her pieces had stickers on them. She floated home. Cory kept an arm around her to keep her from floating off.

CHAPTER 12

How many animals he had at the zoo now, Cory wasn't sure as they were free to come and go as they needed. In the past five months, several new ones had arrived, Cora being the first. Cory was strolling through the park-like estate and stopped now at the crest of the Japanese bridge to survey the vastness everything was still becoming. Ahead of him, the baobab trees stood staunchly in a group and were a nice little walk from the bamboo grove with its meandering paths through shadowed mazes of frothy leaves and stalks.

Somewhere in the middle of them, Ellie was teaching an art class to the visitors he had guided that morning. Cory had shown them the lake and bridge, the baobab trees and, finally, the bamboo grove. Here and there, they had caught glimpses of several of the animals. Connie had even flown in and ridden on his shoulder. After the tour, Cory had taken a solitary stroll to the spring that fed the lake he was standing above. The path always showed itself to him now.

He turned and leaned his back against the rail to better view the forests of immense pines and deciduous hardwoods which rose in the distance behind the house. He could hear a woodpecker in one of the trees and was filled with thankfulness that his path and Ellie's had merged, that they had found their way to their purpose and were living their life's work of guiding people through their illusions and teaching them to see beyond pretentions and seeming separations to the vastness to which everyone and everything is connected.

He remembered when he learned those lessons himself: in the desert, at the ocean, in the cave, at home. He turned back, and leaning his arms on the lacquered rail, he looked across the water through the hazy afternoon light past the end of the lake with its little island to the low, lumpy hills. They were covered now in gold and vermillion and a pumpkiny orange. He looked forward to the alternating browns and whites of the soon approaching winter and looked forward, also, to what Ellie would make with those landscapes.

He raised his gaze past the hills to the desert. He was getting rather fond of it. Every few weeks or so, he hiked out and spend an afternoon or evening hoping to see Ralph. He always took a treat of cheese. More often than not, he was able to give it to Ralph and not just leave it for him. Cory had not been back inside the cave at the desert's western edge. He felt no need though he and Ellie had gone near it one day. They did get to the ocean, but with guiding and teaching and Cory's writing and caring for everything and Ellie's painting and showings, there wasn't as much time as they'd like.

Connie wheeled in and perched on the rail and viewed it all with Cory. "Were you with Ellie's class?" *Yes.* "How are they doing?" *They're coming along.* "Good." *Yes, it is.*

A cold breeze sprang up. "Winter's coming, Connie. I need to ready your indoor/outdoor." *Yes, please. The birdhouse isn't as cozy as I'd like.* "I'll do that this afternoon." *Thank you.* Cory turned in a slow circle, taking in everything—the land, the water, the air—and everywhere—the birds and animals, both the ones that had adopted Cory over the years and the ones that now showed up because of Ellie.

"I need to check on the hive," he looked at Connie. "Want to come along?" *Yes, I think I will.* Cory straightened his back and stepped down from the bridge and started making his way to the back garden.

Ellie found him looking at the empty hive. She slipped her hand into his and looked with him. It's warmer in the desert. I know. They'll be back before you know it. Yah. She squeezed his hand. Like Connie, she's with you all the time. I know; I can feel Zanzibar and the others. Then hold onto that until they return. Cory nodded; I will. I wonder what Zanzibar's true name is. Probably Sophia or something like it. Probably.

CHAPTER 13

Cory felt both elated and a bit unsettled. He had just come from the bee garden. This fall, he'd been able to talk to Zanzibar before she and the bees moved back to the desert for the winter. He was unsettled because, well, he wasn't sure why. Everything seemed to be as it should be, and it wasn't because the bees were leaving. He was used to that now, and Zanzibar told him they'd be back again in the spring. It wasn't as if a trip was coming up. He had not been on one since right before he met Ellie. Connie had not indicated they were necessary right now. With everything else he and Ellie had been learning and doing, he guessed they probably weren't. He knew Connie would let him know if one was needed.

He strolled over to the Japanese bridge to think but stopped short of climbing it to the crest. Not focusing on anything in particular, he let his thoughts roam until he realized it was the little island at the far end of the lake that was calling for his attention. "That's it," he said softly.

Turning from the bridge, he took the dirt path down to the water's edge and stood looking across the lake. From where he stood, he could see the island's general shape and size. He could also make out the shapes of the few trees. Though invisible from where he was, Cory knew it was covered in grass with clumps of low bushes. Large enough to accommodate a small structure and with mostly open space, the island had potential, but getting to it was difficult. Over the years, though, he had made the extra effort, first to row out that far and then to negotiate a landing. The ground was marshy, and there was no beach or even a smooth approach. He always wore chest-high waders and brought an extra-long rope as the trees were farther from the water than he wanted to drag the rowboat. Once on the island, he was on firm ground.

"You're thinking," said Ellie coming alongside him and slipping her hand into his.

"I am."

"About?"

Cory turned to her. "Making a butterfly garden on the little island." He nodded in its direction. "It's the perfect place for one except that the landing's not the easiest."

"No, it's not," Ellie laughed remembering how her waders had filled with water when she tried to get out of the rowboat the first time she went with Cory. "It's a lovely little island though. I can picture a tiny building no more than a hundred square feet or so and mostly open but with the option to have walls in case of rain, a patio, maybe a few more trees, a couple of benches … " Ellie had been pointing out spots where everything could be placed. She stopped when she saw Cory staring at her with his mouth open.

"That's exactly how I see it."

"You haven't done a large project since we built the bee garden. When was that, a little over two years ago?"

"We've been just a bit busy," he said in mock understatement.

"Noooo," Ellie replied and kissed him on the cheek. She looked down at her wedding ring and, scraping a fleck of paint off it, thought of how much had happened in just a couple of years. Meeting each other, making the bee garden, tending the estate, her art shows, Cory's tours, the art classes she was teaching almost every month now, and a year after they met: their wedding.

She hadn't looked through the photos of it in a while. She smiled now at the memory of the ceremony. They stood at the crown of the Japanese bridge. She wore a longer, ivory-colored version of the dress she wore to her first gallery show. Just as she had with that first dress, she placed the little conch shell in its small, secret pocket. Her dark hair was gathered in the chignon Cory especially liked, and she wore a coronet of white flowers interspersed with colorful nasturtiums. Cory, though not crazy about the idea, graciously wore a traditional tuxedo, cummerbund, and bow tie, but he substituted his favorite shirt—cream on cream and western style—for the studded shirt traditionally worn.

"The snaps are just as good as shirt studs," he'd argued.

"I think it's perfect," Ellie had agreed.

His boutonnière was, of course, a daisy.

The ceremony was simple: Connie and Cora, their families flanking them on the bridge, and a dozen close friends. As the ceremony ended, thunder rumbled in the distance, but the rain held off until after a sunset that colored the sky like fireworks. Ellie was reminded of the haiku, "Angels must have been/scribbling on the sky with bright/crayons. The sky laughs." Michel had offered the gallery for their reception. More than fifty friends joined with them to celebrate.

Coming out of her reverie, Ellie said, "Speaking of busy, I'm going to finish getting ready. I need to leave soon for the meet-and-greet."

"Do you need me to come with you?"

"No, you stay and plot. Maybe Connie will join you. I'm sure she likes butterflies, too."

"Okay." Cory turned back to his contemplation. Squinting one eye, he tracked the rim of the lake to the left, past the Japanese bridge and the bamboo grove, and around to where the island sat a good distance from land. He then squinted behind to his right where he caught a glimpse of the birch forest before tracking the lake's rim around to the other side of the island where the gap between it and the land was much narrower.

"Oh," he said, surprised, and looked carefully again. "It needs a bridge," he said as he started back to the house.

Grabbing his keys and phone, he made a quick call and headed into town. After meeting first with one person and then several others, he texted Ellie, "Meet for dinner at Harley's?" Getting her response, he texted back, "6:30 ok?" He grinned.

Cory had just been seated at their favorite window table when he saw her coming up the sidewalk. He always loved watching her walk. Instead of putting one foot in front of the other like everyone else, Ellie seemed to float. He knew she really didn't, but his impression was that she didn't quite touch the ground. This was especially true when she was excited as she seemed to be now. He tapped the window. She turned and, spotting him, broke into a delighted smile. Following her progress to the door, he saw her enter and greet Harold, who led her to their table. Cory already had her chair pulled out.

"Thank you, Harold. Thanks, honey."

"What's up?" asked Cory.

"Well, the meet-and-greet was more interesting than I thought it would be."

"I can see it was important," said Cory nodding to the suit she had chosen to wear. She had left her hair down and now gathered it into an informal ponytail.

"I really hate my hair in my face. Anyway, there were some really big names there. I'm glad I wore a suit. It was all business. Michel's negotiating a commission for me. Guess what it's of," she challenged as she tried not to grin.

"One of the animals?" She shook her head. Occasionally, someone wanted an interpretation of Connie. "The hills with their flowers?"

"Um um," she responded.

"Ralph?"

"Nope."

"The desert, the ocean, the cave?"

She shook her head to each but gave up trying to contain her grin.

"I give up. What could be better than those? The hive!"

"Not that either. Do you remember the collector who bought the landscape of the estate, that large canvas?"

"Of course." Cory wasn't sure how Ellie could top a painting like that. It was the biggest piece she'd ever done. It took her almost ten months to complete.

"He wants a picture of you," she said gleefully.

"Me!" Cory looked horrified at the thought of sitting for it and then knowing his image would be on someone's wall. He started to say, "I don't think I like ..." when Ellie interrupted.

"Baby, do you think I'd agree to anything like that?"

"No," Cory replied blinking. "No, you wouldn't. It just caught me off guard."

"What he wants is you surrounded by your animals. I'm thinking it will be more the impression of you, the, uh, the spiritual you. I was thinking of a medium-sized canvas with you reaching out your arm to Connie who is flying in, and other animals gathered around in a clearing like you see in Christmas cards of St. Nicholas in the forest with woodland creatures."

Cory looked at Ellie as if she'd lost it.

"Don't worry; I'm not nominating you for sainthood or putting you in a red suit."

"Well, that's a relief at least."

"It's more the showing of what a person can do and be when he puts himself in touch with what is infinite and follows his or her higher calling. I think this man is trying very hard to capture for himself what you already know and have. I think he recognizes this at some level but is unaware of what exactly it is you possess that he doesn't. I also think he's very lonely."

She thought a moment. "This isn't the way for him to get what he needs, of course, but having a picture may help him focus his energy in a more useful way. I think he spends all his time running his business, and now he realizes he's missing something. I did stipulate that the two of you must meet so you and he can hammer out the details between what he wants and what you will allow."

Ellie saw him release a deep sigh, "I know I can trust you, but you have to admit it's a very different request."

"I know, but I'm so excited. It's a challenge to walk the tightrope of protecting what you need to have protected and revealing what this man and any other viewer need to see."

Cory nodded and said, "Okay." After a pause, he added, "In fact, I think I'm warming to the idea. I might even be getting a bit excited about it."

"Good. Can you do a 10 o'clock meeting with him and Michel tomorrow morning at the gallery? I left it tentative until I asked you."

Pretty sure he could, Cory checked his schedule anyway. "Yup, that'll work."

"I'll text Michel. Now, what have you been up to?"
Cory's turn, he simply said, "I'm having a bridge built
to the little island."

"What?" Ellie looked around and lowered her voice,
"You're doing what?"

"Yup." Cory looked smug and waited.

"Well, quit holding out. Tell me all about it," she
demanded laughing.

"The path around the lake is an easy stroll, right?" She
nodded. "It's the 50 feet or so of water between it and the island
that's the problem."

"That's for sure," she interrupted.

"There's no good place to store a boat near there, so I
either have to drag the boat down the path every time I want
to go or row almost the entire length of the lake. Either way, I
have to figure out where to land. I thought of making docks
and a small boathouse, but I just don't like that idea. I don't
know why, but it doesn't seem like what needs to be done. I
talked to an architect today who took me to see Kurt Walmsley,
who specializes in small bridges."

"I'm floored," Ellie finally said. "When I said 'project,'
earlier I was thinking you meant the butterfly garden. You
never cease to amaze me."

"I do want to make a butterfly garden, but I, and
anyone helping me make one, need a bridge first. Besides, that
will give me time to learn about butterflies and to plan the
space."

"That makes sense. A companion to the Japanese
bridge?"

Cory looked especially pleased and said, "In a way."
He paused for full effect before adding, "a glass suspension
bridge." Ellie just looked at him, her eyebrows raised. "It's not

all glass, just the bridge deck, and it has steel, uh, trays, I guess you'd call them, to support sections of glass. Here, Kurt made a quick sketch. He used that pic I took of the island a couple months ago when the goldenrod was in bloom."

"I remember," nodded Ellie.

"He's coming out to the estate tomorrow at 1:00." Cory pulled the sketch out of a folder and handed it to Ellie. "I really hope you can meet him."

"Impressive," she remarked after looking it over thoroughly. The sketch showed the island at the left and the path-side of the estate at the right with the water between. Skimming just above the water's surface, and connecting the two pieces of land, was a glass walkway suspended from a delicate-looking lace of shiny, steel cables.

"Kurt is bringing his soil engineer, Mike—I met him, too—with him to assess whether or not the island and mainland can support such a structure. Pylons and anchors have to go deep into the ground. I told them how spongey and marshy the island side is, but they were encouraging." Cory took the sketch back. Ellie watched him look at it. His face shone with anticipation and hope that the project could be brought into being.

"You'll get it done," she said reaching out to rub his fingers.

Cory shrugged, "I hope so. We'll see."

"I like how close to the surface the bridge is and that you'll be able to see through to the water below."

"Me, too. The only time water might submerge it is when there's a strong wind with a storm, and then it's unlikely we'd be out there. Even if we were, the cables act as safety rails."

They excitedly discussed their plans. Deciding to skip coffee and dessert, they went home to stroll over to the Japanese bridge to plan and plot until it got too dark to see.

CHAPTER 14

"What should I wear for this meeting?" Cory called as he looked through his closet the next morning.

"Whatever you feel most comfortable in." He heard the kitchen door shut and then Ellie coming down the hall.

He chose khakis and his favorite shirt, the one he'd worn for their wedding. As he was snapping the cuffs, Ellie appeared in a peasant skirt, jean jacket, and turquoise-studded sandals. Cora was riding in her pocket. "Should I change?" he asked.

"We do look a bit themed, don't we? No, you look nice. I think you set the right tone. I'll change." She kicked her sandals off and traded them for a pair in patent leather. With a black pencil skirt and short jacket, she presented a more urban vibe. "Cora, you'll have to ride in my purse." Cora climbed in atop her wallet. "Are you going to wear cowboy boots?" Ellie teased as Cory finished dressing.

"Nooo, I'm wearing loafers."

Michel's assistant met them at the door and whispered, "He's here already," and rolled his eyes. "They're in the back salon. You look quite chic today, both of you," he added looking from one to the other. "Come. I'll announce you."

Michel saw them before they reached the salon's doorway. "Welcome, welcome. Mr. Brown is here already. Cory, good to see you. It's been a while. You should come more often with Ellie."

Cory wondered at Michel's small talk, something he seldom indulged in. In fact, Michel seemed slightly ill at ease, something else that did not come naturally to him. When Cory turned to greet Mr. Brown, he understood. What struck him first and most was the man's hollowness. That was the only word that came close to the hole in him that needed to be filled. He radiated emptiness and longing, and Cory remembered what Ellie had said yesterday.

Having gotten distracted by a new sculpture, Ellie now appeared and greeted Michel with a quick hug before turning to Mr. Brown. "Good morning, Mr. Brown. I brought someone I thought you might like to meet."

Cory stood back to watch. While he had driven, Ellie and Cora had talked. "Cora, dear, I have a favor to ask of you." *What's that?* "The man we are going to meet is very sad. That's why I especially wanted you to come today. If he has an animal, he doesn't know it. Will you let him pet you?" Cora thought a minute. *That'd be okay.* "Thank you. Here's what I'd like you to do." She coached her until Cora reminded Ellie which one of them was the chipmunk. "True, true, Cora. I'm sorry. You know a lot more about all this than I do. I just feel for him. Work your chipmunk magic."

Ellie helped Cora out of her purse and onto the table. Michel invited them to sit down. Mr. Brown seemed entranced with Cora and tentatively reached his hand out palm up. Cora sat down, looked at him, looked around, scratched an ear, and when Mr. Brown started to pull his hand back, she calmly skipped over and climbed into it. The look of astonishment and wonder on the man's face momentarily transformed him, and in that moment, Ellie captured the essence of what she wanted her painting to show.

I've grown so used to Cory I've forgotten how empty and unaware so many people are, she thought as she made mental notes and quick sketches. Mr. Brown went so far as to make a nest of his hands where Cora contentedly curled up until Michel offered drinks and brought out a small dish of water for her.

Excusing himself a moment, Michel returned with a marigold in his button hole for Cora to find. This was an ongoing game between them, but today's placement was easy. She scampered over, tugged it out and took it to where Ellie was sitting in an easy chair off to the side. Without a pocket to climb into, though, she had to content herself with the upholstered arm of the chair. Mr. Brown watched, fascinated.

After more small talk, mostly about Cora, Michel began his mediation. Used to Cora's presence and always glad when Ellie brought her, Michel had relaxed, and the meeting was progressing smoothly. As the men conducted their business, Ellie captured the impressions she wanted for later use. Cory's quiet confidence and his open, straightforward manner always drew people to him. It was no different for Mr. Brown. Between Cora and Cory, Mr. Brown's anxious vibrations had slowed enough where they no longer filled the room like a sour, overpowering cologne. As Michel asked questions to set the boundaries of each man's expectations, Ellie continued to sketch and take notes.

Finally, feeling she needed to simply look on for a bit, she closed her sketch pad and broke down the scene in front of her. Using a technique she often employed to remove herself and her prior knowledge from what she was viewing, she breathed deeply several times and thought, I'm on a sidewalk, and I stop to look in through a large window. What do I see?

She began the list. Three men sit around a table, which is round so none of them has the advantage of placement to seem more important than the others. The table is small enough that all three have to be sociable or take the chance of seeming to be rude.

One man, we'll call him "Leader," obviously has a different role than the other two as both of them look at him when he talks, but he does not necessarily look at them when they talk. He sits straight and firm—grounded—and looks expectantly but nonjudgmentally at one man and then the other. He's dressed professionally in a Saville-row suit with a gold-colored square in the breast pocket, a white shirt, and apricot- and maroon-colored tie. His dress seems to say he chose them because he likes them, and it doesn't matter to him if you do or not. His attitude also seems apparent in his hair, which is a mane of silver that is combed back from his forehead and descends neatly almost to his collar where it curls and gets a bit unruly. When Leader stops talking, the man he's looking at starts.

The man talking now, we'll call him "Suit," is dressed in a well-tailored, dark suit and a power tie, but he looks anything but powerful. Suit's shoulders sag and the padding in the jacket can't hide that though he seems to hope it will. His hair is cut perfectly and his nails are groomed, but in contrast to Leader, it's as if he's pleading to be accepted. That's interesting; he seems to need acceptance from both everyone else as well as from himself. He leans forward overly eager to please in contrast to the impression his suit, haircut, and—Ellie glanced under the table—highly polished oxfords are trying to make. It's all surface. I wonder if it fools anyone. It doesn't seem to fool Leader, and it also doesn't seem to matter to him either.

The third man, we'll call him "Mensch," seems relaxed and interested in the conversation. He leans slightly forward as he talks and gestures with one, and sometimes both, hands. When he listens, he leans back with his arms relaxed at his sides. He's dressed in a refreshing and endearing mix of western shirt, khakis and loafers. His hair needs a trim. The cowlick at the back is beginning to stick up. This is where trying to be objective about Cory always fell apart. Ellie petted Cora a moment and refocused. Mensch exudes as much gentle, positive energy as Suit exudes anxiety and sadness ... and submerged anger. I didn't notice that at first. I'm glad we're doing this project, thought Ellie as she tuned back in to the conversation. Michel seemed to be wrapping up.

"Are you both in agreement with those points?"

Both men said, "yes."

"Good. This is what I also heard. Cory, you are willing to have a likeness of yourself and any of your animals included in whatever forms and ways Ellie chooses to present you and them." Cory nodded.

"Mr. Brown, you wish Cory's likeness to be included in whatever form Ellie deems appropriate and as many animals to be depicted as the artist deems appropriate, but you have no preference about the background. As well, you stipulate that an eagle is to be included."

"Yes," responded Mr. Brown.

Michel turned to Ellie. "Are these parameters acceptable, especially the eagle?" Ellie nodded. Michel continued, "The canvas size is to be between two by three feet to two-and-one-half by four feet. Is this acceptable?"

"I can work within all those boundaries, yes."

Michel turned back to include the men. "I'll have my lawyer draw up the contract. I will send previews to all of you. Then, Mr. Brown, I will have my notary arrange a time for him to bring you a copy. If you could have a witness present and would sign it in his presence so he can bring it back, I would appreciate it. Cory, Ellie, I assume you can stop by the gallery to sign it." They all agreed.

After the men said their formal goodbyes, Mr. Brown stopped by Ellie's chair to pet Cora. After he left, Ellie said, "I'm so glad we're doing this."

"Me, too," replied Cory.

Michel looked quizzically at him. "I thought I'd get more of a fuss from you about having your image on canvas."

"We talked about it, and I trust Ellie."

They chatted as they went into the gallery. Ellie wanted to know about the new statue: a middle-aged couple dancing naked. The couple did not have dancers' bodies, far from it. They had middle-aged bodies that showed how years of use and good food had rounded and softened them, but they were dancing with joy and abandon as if they didn't care who might see them.

"Ellie, honey, I need to get back to prepare for Kurt's visit."

"Oh, that's right. Cory's planning a glass bridge," she informed Michel.

"Of course, he is," was all Michel could think to say.

CHAPTER 15

Ellie needed a break from the painting. She was satisfied with its progress. She just needed to step away for an hour or two. Not finding Cory in his office, she checked the fridge for a note and then wandered out to the front porch. Hearing the rude noises of a large truck backing up, she remembered it was Day One, the day construction was to begin on the bridge's supports. Two huge trucks were lumping down the path. She could see exhaust from the noisy one, which was already at the lake. Picking up her small sketch pad and pencil case, she made her way along the path until it was blocked by the two trucks jockeying for position. Ellie looked into the underbrush and tree tops and farther into the edge of a small woods and wondered what the animals thought of the noise and disruption. As far away as the old forest was, she was pretty sure the engines and grinding gears could be heard there, too.

Cory spotted her and was making his way around the idling trucks, "Hey there!" he said fondly. "Come on."

He took her hand and led her around the trucks as a man Ellie didn't know yelled, "Watch out. People walking," to the drivers, who acknowledged with raised hands.

"Ellie, this is Mike. He's the soil engineer. Mike, my wife, Ellie."

"Glad to meet you. What do you think?" he asked beaming.

"I think it's fabulous," Ellie shouted as one of the trucks backed up. "So, it's going to work? Not too spongy?"

The truck noises lessened to a dull thrum as they again idled, waiting for the crews to harness the bridge supports to the crane. "Nah, piece of cake. We've built successfully on ground a lot less firm. What you have is just soggy on top. Deeper, it's quite stable. The foundations are there to stay."

Cory's excitement radiated from him, and Ellie was thrilled for him. "I think I'll go back now," she shouted as all three trucks roared into full volume again.

"Put these on."

"What?"

Cory handed her the set of earmuffs he was holding, said something to Mike and, catching Ellie's attention, gestured back down the path. Ellie nodded and followed. When they were far enough away to be able to hear each other, she handed the earmuffs back and said, "I'll watch from a distance."

"I have an extra set of earmuffs. It has a headset in it, too." He was clearly enthralled with the entire process.

"That's okay. I'll go to the Japanese bridge. I can see from there and sketch."

"All right. I'll probably be out here all day."

"Of course. You enjoy the experience; I'll record it." She stroked his cheek before heading back down the path.

"Hi Cora," she said as she opened her sketch pad and rested it on the bridge rail. *It's too noisy over there.* "Yes, but that's how some things get done." *I know, but none of us like it.* "I'm sure. I don't either."

Connie flew in and perched on the lacquered rail. "Hey, Connie." Ellie noticed other animals peeking through foliage and underbrush. She heard Berkeley high in the sky and remarked, "Berkeley has the best view and probably a lot less noise." *It won't last all that long*, replied Connie. "You're right. It won't. You animals are all being very calm about it." *It's what we do.* Ellie heard Cory's bullfrog, new to the estate, croaking from the reeds near where the rowboat was tied.

Abruptly, she looked up from her pad and took in the scene in front of her. The position of the animals came into focus. "That's what the painting needs," she whispered to herself. She turned the paper to a fresh page and quickly sketched an eagle high in the sky, various animals half hidden in the background, Connie and Cora near her, and a snail at her feet just because she liked it there. After watching the crane hoist part of a support and one of the crews position it and begin to fix it in place, Ellie decided her break was over.

Walking into the studio, she ignored the canvas until she'd put her pencil case away and had turned the pad to the animal sketch she'd just made. Only then did she look at the canvas and mentally overlay the sketch. "Yes," she nodded to herself and began to add the animals peeking from their protective foliage.

*   *   *

Before the crane started hoisting the first support, Mike got Cory's attention and indicated a knoll a distance from the main action. "We need to get out of the crew's way now. Eddie doesn't need to be thinking about where we are," he said as they made themselves comfortable on the grass.

"Are soil engineers always involved in this part of the process?" asked Cory worried he was here because he thought something might go wrong.

Mike gave him an embarrassed grin, "Nah, I just like construction. My favorite toy as a kid was a dump truck." They watched quietly for a bit. Then, Mike asked, "This is quite an estate. How did, I mean, where did it all?" He stopped. "I don't even know how to ask the question. How does someone build something like this?"

This was one of Cory's favorite questions. "Everyone has the capability inside them to do what they are meant to do, to become who they are meant to be, and to offer their particular talents. How was it all built? By people like you. I can see it, but I can't make it happen by myself. You, Eddie, the crews, Kurt, and Yoshio, who introduced me to Japanese architecture and installed the other bridge—you brought it into being. Of course, many of the trees were already here, but I planted more than a few and moved my fair share of rocks. So, we all made it happen."

"What about the animals? How did you get them?"

"They come on their own." Mike looked confused. Cory continued, "We draw to us who and what we need. I don't procure animals. I accept those who show up." He told him about Connie.

Mike looked skeptical but not as if Cory was crazy. "I can see that would be an interesting way to do things. Makes it difficult to plan though. First pylon's down. Let's go see."

Sunlight glinted off the metal tower. "It's a lot smaller than I thought it would be," remarked Cory trying not to be disappointed.

"That's only the bottom part. They have to put it up in sections" Cory nodded his understanding. "Besides," Mike added, "most of the structure is below grade. As the bridge is for foot traffic, you don't need a huge tower above grade, but they aren't finished. It'll be a work in progress for a couple of days."

"I think I'm going to like it," said Cory.

They moved off again as the crews readied the crane and second pylon base. This one, on the island side, was trickier because of the water expanse. Crews had built temporary scaffolding to help them maneuver the pylon onto its foundation. "This one will take longer," said Mike. "It's been a pleasure, but I have a meeting," he yelled as the deafening roar began again. Cory quickly put his earmuffs back on as did Mike, who waved his farewell.

Cory sat happily watching the trucks, the metal swinging from the end of the crane, the men doing their jobs. He ate the sandwich he'd brought with him. At the end of the day, he walked back with them to their pickups, which were parked at the entrance.

"How early is too early tomorrow?" asked Eddie.

"Any time after it gets light," Cory replied.

"Okay. We'll see you about 7:00."

Before going back into the house, Cory looked back towards the lake to the last of the sunlight glinting off the shining metal. He shook his head with awe at the thought of bringing something like this into being.

He found Ellie in the living room with her feet up, a cup of tea and a book. "Are you sick?" he asked in mock confusion.

"I know! No, I got to a stopping place on the canvas and want to let the images gel in my brain a bit. I'll probably work into the night. How's the bridge coming along?"

"Great. The pylons, or at least parts of them, are in place. On both sides," he added. "It's amazing to watch. A completely different process than installing the Japanese bridge was. Am I allowed to see the painting?"

"Sure." Ellie swung her feet off the ottoman and followed Cory into her studio.

"It's not at all what I thought it would be," he said as he looked at it all left to right, back left, and then top to bottom and back to the top.

"You're doing what I keep doing," said Ellie as she watched him.

"What's that?"

"You're looking at it directionally: back and forth both directions and up and down."

Cory paused. "I am, aren't I? How's that different from how people usually look at a picture?"

"People usually first take in the whole and then move to details that particularly interest them."

Cory thought back. He'd seen a lot of art since meeting Ellie. "You're right. Why's this one different?"

"I'm not sure. Maybe we're looking for particular animals?"

"The background is darker at the left and gets increasingly lighter towards the right. The animals are easier to see at the right, too."

"How do you feel about the way I presented you?"

He nodded and smiled. "I like it. I'm me but not where people will say, 'Isn't that that animal-zoo-estate guy?' They'll probably think I'm just some dude who needs a haircut. The animals take center stage."

"Good, that's what I intended. I did paint you in your favorite shirt."

"Oh, yah, I see. Thanks. I just better not wear it to the opening."

"It's going into his private collection. I'm not sure he'll even show it."

"Even better." They started out of the studio. "The crew is coming at 7:00. Oh," Cory stopped as he realized. "I'm sorry. You just said you'll be painting late. I'll call them to start later."

"No, it's okay. You can't have them waste daylight. It's okay," she said again as Cory looked annoyed with himself. "Sometimes working on little sleep actually helps me see things I wouldn't if I'd gotten a whole night's worth. I think I'll call my mom and see if she wants to do lunch tomorrow. In fact, I think I'll take a short nap now," she said as she took off her shoes and stretched out on the sofa.

Cory tucked the throw around her. "I'll leave you some supper in the fridge."

"Thanks, honey," she replied drowsily.

Ellie awoke about 8 p.m. feeling much clearer about the details she'd been struggling with. She thought about the directional scanning Cory had done when he looked at it and wondered if other people would do the same and what it meant if they did. She called her mom, invited her to lunch and asked if she could pick her up. After making a large cup of tea and grabbing the sandwich Cory had made her, she headed back into the studio. She studied her work a moment before smiling, satisfied. The painting now seemed to be headed in a direction of wholeness. The epiphany she'd had on the bridge was what it had needed. She knew now how to finish it and readied herself for a long night of work.

CHAPTER 16

After a short night of sleep, Ellie was busy painting when she heard a car door shut. "Hi, Mom. I want you to see something before we go to lunch."

"Okay. How are you, sweetie?"

Ellie led her to the studio and then entered first so she could gauge her mother's reaction. "Oh, Ellie. You never let me see an unfinished painting. How special." Ellie watched. Yes, her mother did the same thing: left to right and back, up, then down and back up.

"Can you describe to me how you are viewing it?"

"Ah, a quiz. Now I know why you are letting me see it. Give me a minute." She looked carefully at it again.

"I see the dark and the light. I can see animals in the light part, but I have to look carefully to see them in the darker parts. I like that little snail. He has a companion in the, is that an eagle in the sky? It's so tiny. There aren't many other animals on the ground. They all seem to be half hidden. I do like how you painted Cory. I'm surprised he let you," she finished.

"Thanks, Mom. It's a commission. The buyer wanted Cory and his animals. Cory's seen it and is okay with it."

"I'm what? Oh, hi, Melinda," he said coming in to hug his mother-in-law. They started chatting about the painting, but a loud "pop" made them all jump. "This is the next phase of the bridge. Gotta go." Cory kissed Ellie and Melinda and hurried out, grabbing his travel bag and, at the last minute, the earmuffs.

"What bridge?" asked Melinda turning to Ellie.

"I'll tell you about it on the way. This is why we aren't having lunch here."

Putting on the earmuffs as he headed around the house, Cory could hear Eddie talking to one of the crew bosses. This was Day Two, the big day for the pylons to be finished and the start of what Cory thought of as the actual bridge: anchoring and stringing the wire cables and laying the bridge deck. He had planned to spend the entire day watching the installation, but not long into the morning, he felt he should check on Ralph and Zanzibar and as many of the other animals as he could get to without being gone overnight.

He had enlisted Connie and Cora to take messages to the more remote parts of the estate. He now walked around to the bee garden. He didn't expect them to be back from the desert as it wasn't yet Equinox, but he went just to make sure. The hive was empty, and the trees and bushes only held unfurled buds. He made his way around to where he kept the rowboat. Even the bullfrog was quiet. "Sorry," he called. "The noise will be over soon, probably tomorrow or the next day; well, the worst of it," he amended.

Cory checked that he'd put Ralph's cheese in the bag. It was a smaller version of the bag he'd taken to the desert. He had made the second bag when he started taking day trips. The larger bag was perfect for a trip of several days, but there was no reason to lug around something heavier than he needed for a morning or afternoon. He was about to head across the hills to the desert's eastern edge where he usually found Ralph, but something told him to head to the ocean and enter at the desert's southern edge. He backtracked and took off around the far end of the bamboo grove. Within a half hour, he was standing on the beach. The surf was a continuous, soothing flow rolling up and back, up and back.

As Cory watched the surf and thought about how he had discovered he had an ocean, Connie fluttered onto the bench. Ellie had wanted it since she saw it in a store across from Michel's gallery and had bought it after her first show. It was for a remembrance of their first meeting, she had said. Cory thought she just didn't like sitting on sand.

"Hey, Connie. How's it going?" *The noise isn't bad in the old forest, but I told one of the snails. I found the blue jay, and she'll tell everyone in the new forest.* "Thanks, Connie. I'll bet you're tired." *A bit. I didn't get out to the desert.* "That's okay. I'm heading there now." *I'll ride along.* "Great! I'd love to have your company. I assume Berkeley has told the other birds, but I haven't seen Cora." *She went to the hills to spread the word.*

Instead of walking on the packed sand near the surf, Cory turned north, directly into the desert. By adjusting his direction a bit to the east, he skirted the rise he'd so laboriously climbed and then rolled down on that first trip. He now doubled back to the bottom of the rise and set out for the clump of bushes where he'd eaten his lunch that first day and where he had also left the yellow pebble. Sitting in the shade of the largest bush, as if waiting for him, was Ralph.

"Did you know I was coming?" asked Cory astonished. Ralph got up and looked hopeful. Cory lowered himself to the ground and skootched under the shade of the bush. "Hey, Ralph. How are you?" Ralph seemed pleased to see him and let Cory pat him, but abruptly moved off, not far, just enough to say he was done with being petted. "All right. I brought you cheese." Ralph licked his nose and watched intently as Cory unwrapped it. When he held it out, Ralph took it carefully from him and, lying back down, ate it within reach of Cory. Well, that's progress, thought Cory.

"You may have heard all the noise," he began and told Ralph about the bridge. "Will you pass it on to any animals that might want to know? It won't last more than another day or so." Ralph looked him in the eye, blinked a combination yes and thank-you-for-the-cheese and then loped off. *Not much for conversation, is he?* commented Connie. "No, not much. I do so like Ralph," said Cory as he dusted sand off his jeans and headed in the direction of the cave.

They were half way there when Connie said, *Look behind you.* Cory didn't even have to look to know she meant bees. He put his arms out as he turned. Soon, he was covered. "Hi, Zanzibar. I wanted to explain about the noise." *Yes, we noticed.* "It will be over soon. I'm having a bridge built to make getting to the little island easier." *We'll move back when it gets quiet.* "I'll look for you in a week or so, then."

Cory strolled back home and entered through the side door, the one nearest Ellie's studio, but she wasn't there. Hearing noises in the kitchen, he found her making pasta. "Don't you ever work on the painting anymore?"

"Nope, gave it up, decided to spend all my time cooking and napping. How are the animals?"

"They're all okay. Ralph let me pat him a little."

"Really? Wow!"

"Yah, just a little, but still. How is the painting?"

"It's coming along. I don't want you to see it again for a bit."

"Okay." Cory knew that meant she needed a holiday reaction. Early on, Ellie had explained that it was like the difference in seeing a child every day versus just on holidays— the longer the time between seeing it, the more chance there was that certain things would stand out. "I'm going to check on the project."

"All right. Dinner should be ready in about an hour."

Cory got to the bridge as the crews were getting ready to leave. He walked back with them to the entrance. The trucks lumped on ahead, their noise-makers silent now that their part of the job—and all the backing up—was over. "Thank you so much," said Cory shaking hands with the workers. He climbed up the outside of the truck cabs to shake hands with the drivers. Kurt and Mike had come out earlier and now caught up with the group.

"Thanks, Eddie," Kurt called. Eddie nodded and waved as he directed the crews off the estate. "I think this will be one of my favorites," said Kurt turning to Cory and Mike. "The cable and deck crews should be able to finish in the next few days. I'd like to send my photographer out after that."

"Of course," replied Cory pulling out one of his cards. "Just ask him to give me 24 hours' notice if he can."

"Will do."

Ellie had come out and walked over to them. "Doesn't it look great? A nice balance to the Japanese bridge." They all looked over to the Japanese bridge off to their left and from it to the new bridge off to their right in the distance. The soft luster of the Japanese bridge was the moon to the new bridge's shiny, metallic sun though in many respects the bridges were similar. The Japanese bridge, with its traditional rainbow curve, was lacquered in umber with glints of oranges and reds. The new bridge, which Cory had christened the butterfly bridge, would in a few days have a bowl-like curve in shiny silvers. Both had intricate supports, and both offered solid, though very different, foundations and a means to one's destination. "They're perfect together."

"Yes, they are," agreed Kurt. "I should hire Cory to design. He had the vision."

Cory blushed and said, "I don't think I could repeat it on command. It just seemed what it needed to be for my purpose."

CHAPTER 17

It was now several weeks into spring. Cory's projects on the island and Ellie's painting were both nearing completion. Zanzibar had brought the bees back, and Cory invited her out to see the finished bridge. *It's lovely, Cory. I'll bring the bees out tomorrow to see it. They'll appreciate having a colony of butterflies nearby.* "I'm glad you approve. You know a lot more about butterflies than I do. Any advice?" She hovered in front of him. *You did a wonderful work in our garden. I think you'll do just fine here, too.* "Thank you. That means so much, especially coming from you."

Ellie strolled out to the island almost daily during the last few weeks before completing the painting. The bridge deck felt solid underfoot, but she still got a bit giddy as if she were actually walking on the water. She assumed she would grow used to the feeling and quit having it soon though she hoped not. She liked the surreal thrill when she first looked down and saw the water inches below her.

Cory spent most of his time working on the island. Sometimes, he went out with Ellie but stayed on his own when she needed to go back to painting. Sometimes, he took a specialist with him for advice about plants, habitat, structures, and anything else he needed to learn.

Progress seemed slow, but soon a small structure took shape. Not quite a gazebo and not quite a garden shed, it fit in perfectly. The last task was to lay a flagstone patio between the structure and the butterfly habitat. After several weeks of long days, Cory was able to say the work on the island was done except for choosing a finish for the structure. On the last afternoon, Cory helped Jason Levine install a driftwood and ceramic fountain in the patio area.

"I can't thank you enough for this fountain, Jason. It's perfect," said Cory as they watched the water fall from pan to pan into a small, glazed basin.

"I'm so happy you like it." Jason's face was shining. "I know you like driftwood, and I was glad to do it for you. It's meant a lot to me, Cory, yours and Ellie's friendship."

"Come back to the house with me, and let's see if she'll let us in the studio."

"I'd love to, but I have a meeting in town." On their way back to the house, they stopped at a crescent-shaped area Cory had cleared between the path and the lake. Equidistant from both bridges, it had the best view of them. Cory had set several benches along the curve facing the lake side. Depending on where they chose to sit, visitors could enjoy the view of one or both bridges. Jason looked from one to the other. "Each bridge is marvelous on its own. Together, they make something very special."

"I think so, too. Somehow, they seem to be more together than they are on their own. I haven't quite figured it out yet."

Jason nodded. "I know what you mean." He checked his phone. "Oh, I'll be late if I don't get going." They walked back to the house where they parted ways at the drive.

Ellie was cleaning brushes when she heard Cory come in. "It's finished," she called, jubilant.

"Can I see it now?" he called eagerly as he waited outside the studio door in case he wasn't supposed to go in yet.

He heard Ellie moving around, "Yes, you can come in."

Cory entered and looked for her easel. Usually in the middle of the room, it was now positioned under the largest window. As he walked to it, his gaze shifted across the canvas from left to right, back and forth. "Are they all there?" he asked in awe as he stopped a few feet in front of it.

"The impressions of them are," answered Ellie.

"I can see Hank in there, too. Hi, Hank," he whispered. He backed up and looked at Ellie. "How do you do that? How do you make me see dozens of animals?" He glanced again at the painting. "I can only see some of them now."

"It's a matter of perspective," shrugged Ellie.

"It's marvelous," Cory said putting his arm around her.

"I'm glad you like it, but I'm also glad it's finished."

"The island is, too, well, close enough. Wait 'til you see the fountain Jason made. It's amazing."

"You want to go back out there now?"

"How about after dinner? I'm hungry."

"Harley's?"

"Of course. We need to celebrate."

"Oh, we should. Let's have a party."

"Oh, I meant you and me at Harley's, but a party would be fun."

As they ate and planned, they discussed how they wanted people to see the bridge and the painting. "I don't want this to be like guiding groups on tours."

"I agree. It should be informal, a party. A small one, I think."

"Like our wedding ceremony was."

"Exactly!" said Ellie. "I know you want to tell people about the bridge while they're seeing it, and I want to watch people's reactions to the painting."

After some discussion, they decided Cory would take no more than five people at a time out to the bridge, while Ellie invited everyone else into the studio. As people came back from the bridge, Cory would take another group out until everyone who wanted to had seen it.

"I think I call that a plan," said Ellie tossing her napkin on the table.

"Me, too."

"When do you want to have the party?" Ellie asked. "I need to take the painting to Mr. Brown in about four weeks."

"How about the evening before?"

"I'm excited. We haven't hosted a party in ages. Now, can we go see Jason's fountain?"

CHAPTER 18

The evening before Ellie took the painting to the gallery, they hosted their families and a dozen or so friends including Jason and Michel. The invitation read

Please join us at The Estate
for a private viewing of *Journey*
and a tour of the Butterfly Bridge.
We recommend you wear flat shoes.
Tours begin at 4 pm. Buffet supper at 6 pm.

Ellie had asked Michel if he could arrive early. She heard his vintage T-bird and went out to greet him. Michel put up a hand, "Don't say anything until I've seen it." When he entered the studio, he stopped a distance from where Ellie had placed her show easel in the middle of the room. Cory had helped her adjust the lighting for maximum effect. A viewer could see into the dark areas but had to work a bit to see what might be there. In the lighter areas, everything was clearly visible.

Ellie watched Michel closely. His eyes immediately went to the left where he noticed Cory. He gave a short laugh, "I'm sure it made him happy that he's in his wedding shirt. I don't really take him in though. I'm more interested in following the path he's on and in finding the animals."

Maybe that's it, thought Ellie. People are following the path from dark to light while concentrating on the animals. She lost track of Michel's monologue as she thought about paths and how they figured in her works. The path in this painting was incidental, simply what Cory and the animals would naturally follow, but maybe it took on a special importance to other viewers.

"I'm sorry, Michel, you were saying?"

"The painting is almost set up like a compass. It has the west-east, horizontal dimension of—I'll call it daily existence—the things we simply do, and the south-north, vertical dimension of the things we strive for spiritually. The decoration throughout, in this case, the animals, represents the best in ourselves, what we can bring out with a little work. Remember when we met, and I told you your pieces show what our souls know to be true?"

Ellie nodded.

He held a hand out to the painting, "You've provided a way for us to see into our souls if we'll just look."

"I hadn't thought of it that way. I didn't even plan it that way." She told him about standing on the Japanese bridge on Day One and seeing the vision of the whole painting. As she finished her story, she added, "and it started with placing Cory off to the side so he'd be there as Mr. Brown wanted but not front and center as Cory would have hated. At first, I likened my vision to those depictions of Santa in a snowy forest surrounded by woodland creatures, but then it progressed to Cory in the shadows with his animals projected out around him. I didn't want it to just be a picture of a man who already has animals. I wanted to show Mr. Brown all the good things he can have, too." She laughed, "I guess that is really the same thing you said except you said it much better."

"And you've done that. You've given him a way to see. I'm not sure what he's going to think, though, of the eagle and the snail, especially," Michel pointed to the little snail by Cory's foot."

"When my mom asked what was in the sky, I enlarged the eagle so it's clearly an eagle, and I added its shadow near the snail. I just like the snail, and they're good energy. To my knowledge, Cory doesn't have a snail." Ellie added, "Well, most of the animals aren't Cory's. I mean they are because Cory looks after them, but many show up because of the people who visit. They're here for them rather than for Cory or me. I hope Mr. Brown understands this."

They were interrupted by the sounds of cars pulling in. Michel said he'd stay in the studio. Ellie went outside to help Cory greet their guests. Cory's family arrived at pretty much the same time, so he took them out first. Ellie could see them stop midway between the two bridges and walk out into the crescent. She smiled fondly as she watched Cory gesturing while he talked. She knew he was giving them the opportunity to see how the bridges fit with one another and with the landscape as a whole.

As Ellie propped the side door open and placed the "This way to the Studio" sign by it, Jason pulled up. "Jason, I'm so glad you could make it. I wasn't sure when I got your text."

"Me, either," he said giving her a hug. "Traffic wasn't nearly as bad as the road reports made it sound." He stopped and looked around. Ellie could see his shoulders relaxing. "That's such a beautiful bridge!"

Ellie was about to say, "And your fountain invites people onto the island," when she realized he was looking off to the left. "You've been to it, haven't you, when you've visited?"

"Yes, I've been a number of times. I never get tired of it."

"Cory doesn't either. It's his go-to thinking spot. Yoshio installed it himself, well, with help, of course."

"Yoshio?"

"Oh, Cory lived in Japan for more than a year and studied the Japanese aesthetic under Yoshio Haruko."

"He didn't tell me that."

"He's pretty modest."

Jason was still looking back and forth between the bridges. "It's the combination of shape and color on the Japanese bridge and how it blends with its surroundings, and then … to look across to the butterfly bridge, which looks not quite real, like a sculpture of steel lace. The juxtaposition is incredible. Two different worlds that blend seamlessly."

"Why don't you go out and enjoy them?" She watched until Jason stopped at the crescent then turned her attention to the guests who'd just arrived.

Ellie had placed a few small paintings, mostly of the animals, around the studio's perimeter and had collected her pre-painting sketches and inspirations on the far-end wall. Several people had gathered at the drawings and were pointing to different animals. She heard Cory's mom giggle as she looked at the drawings of Cory. I need to give her whichever one she likes best, thought Ellie making a mental note to remember to do that before Diane left.

In between going out to greet guests and welcoming people back from the bridge, Ellie watched people's reactions to the painting. She knew Michel was, too. Most visitors scanned the painting as she, Cory, her mom, and Michel had. A few viewed it as most people do any painting. Ellie wasn't sure if that said something about the viewer or the painting. As she brought Jeana and Derek in, she heard someone say, "I really like that little snail for some reason." Another responded, "Me, too. It just seems so hopeful."

After most everyone had seen the painting, Michel asked Cory to show him the bridge. Cory looked to see if Michel was wearing his usual Italian-made shoes and was surprised. "You're wearing cross trainers!" he remarked.

"You said to wear something solid," replied Michel.

As they set out, Cory did not act as guide but, rather, simply accompanied him. Michel strolled slowly and stopped often. Cory wondered how he could get more visitors to relax and notice as Michel was doing.

When they got past the last curve in the path and could see the bridge deck, Michel laughed. "It's genius, Cory." He stopped about halfway across the decking to survey the water beneath, the lake stretching out to the left until it narrowed near the Japanese bridge and disappeared near the bamboo grove, and the little island in front of him. He headed to the patio. "Jason's fountain looks very much at home here."

"Yes, it does."

"It's a brighter palette for him." He looked at Cory. "He wouldn't let me see it until I saw it here for myself. It complements the flagstones and this." Michel gestured to the structure. "It's like a gazebo but with the capability of having solid walls." He walked around it thoughtfully and then went inside to inspect the interior structure.

"In case of rain or wind, or even snow. I knew it needed walls but wasn't sure how to pull it off, so I contacted Yoshio, who mailed a set of plans."

"The kind of problem he solves so well."

"He's trying to schedule a visit in the fall."

"Let me know when. We'll make time for him to come to the gallery."

"Absolutely. He'll probably bring it up before I have a chance to mention it." Cory showed Michel how the folding walls worked. "I just need to get a finish on them, and they'll last for years. I'm making a waterproof chest that will double as storage for garden implements as well as seating."

"You're a good planner, Cory. What about the butterflies?"

"I'm hoping some will take up residence by next summer. There's still too much work and noise here right now. And, anyway, that's up to the butterflies. I don't procure animals."

Michel nodded, remembering Ellie telling him that. "I could stay all evening even without butterflies, but I suppose we should go back." He stopped again on the bridge. "I hope Ellie paints this. I'd like to buy it."

Harley's catered supper. Ellie had scattered side tables throughout the living and dining rooms, and Cory had moved the tiled tables from the porch and placed them in the studio. People either wandered with their plates or sat and chatted. Ellie and Cory carried their plates and spent most of their time answering questions. Towards the end of the evening, Ellie found Diane and took her over to the sketches of Cory.

"What do you think?"

"They are all so much him, but I really like this one," she said, pointing to a charcoal sketch that showed Cory with a look that said he was planning. "It reminds me of when he was a boy plotting funeral pyres for his stuffed animals. He drove me nuts with those fires. He was always careful though."

"He still plots and plans," said Ellie, "and he's still careful. He's such a good man."

"I love this one," Diane said pointing to the one done in pastels of Cory looking at Connie, who was sitting on his finger. He had his arm raised so he and Connie were eye to eye. The look on his face was of sheer joy and awe.

Ellie pulled them down, signed them, and handed them to Diane. "They're yours. Let me find a folder for them."

"Oh, Ellie, thank you. They're so special. Dan, look what Ellie gave us," she said as Cory's dad walked up to them.

"How nice. Thank you, Ellie." He gave his daughter-in-law a hug. "But your painting. It's really ... I can't even describe how it makes me feel. I hope the owner loans it to a museum."

"I'm not sure he will. He already owns the largest canvas I've ever done, and he didn't show it, but who knows?"

Guests started saying their goodbyes. Michel was hanging back, waiting. "Can we talk a moment before I go?"

"Of course," said Ellie leading the way to the living room and more comfortable chairs than the studio offered. She was pretty sure he wanted to prep her for tomorrow's meeting with Mr. Brown.

"Me, too?" asked Cory.

"Of course," Ellie and Michel said simultaneously.

Michel began, "You both know me. You know I am on your side." Ellie began to wonder where this was going. "The painting is rich with meaning. It draws the viewer in and suggests possibilities for him to consider. Some viewers will feel invited. Others will feel challenged. Mr. Brown is a proud man, and I don't think he is expecting what you are bringing him tomorrow. I think he will feel challenged, but, more than that, I think he may feel intimidated. He may make a fuss. You know how to handle fusses, Ellie. I just want you to be prepared. We have a contract if it comes to that." Michel saw that, though they both looked a bit shocked, Ellie especially seemed to be taking it well.

"Now, after saying all that, I don't want you spending the night worrying. You saw and heard how well it was received this evening. I know they were all family and friends, but they could have whispered behind your back or while you were out of the room. I listened and watched carefully. They responded to the help and the hope the animals offer. Some of them even seemed to understand the eagle's placement and the presence of the snail. I could see them put themselves in place of Cory. As a painting, it's a total success. As a commission, we may have a little work to do."

"Thank you, Michel," said Ellie as they walked him to his car. "We'll just see what happens tomorrow."

"Yes we will. See you at 10:00," said Michel as he waved his goodbye.

Enough light lingered that they were able to make out both bridges. Cory was looking from one to the other. When Ellie saw him break into a grin and nod, she asked, "What are you thinking?"

"I know now how to finish the gazebo and the folding walls. I need to see if the guy that lacquered the bridge can do them to match."

"Oh, Cory, that will be beautiful and restful for the butterflies … if butterflies care," she laughed. "You know what I mean. What about adding polished metal lanterns on the supports?"

"I like that." Cory described his vision, and Ellie made several more suggestions until it was truly night and too dark to see either bridge. "We'd better get some sleep. If Michel is right, we'll need to be rested for tomorrow." Ellie nodded and then sighed but with fingers crossed, always with fingers crossed and a prayer for all to be as it should be.

CHAPTER 19

They drove to the gallery's loading entrance where Michel's assistant was waiting for them. " I can't wait to see it," he said, always excited when Ellie brought new paintings.

He wheeled it carefully to the salon, unwrapped it and, placing it on the easel, stood back. All he could do was shake his head. "This one just might be my favorite."

"You always say that, Alonzo," said Ellie laughing.

"But it's true. You either get better and better, I don't see how, or I get better at understanding them," he replied.

"Well, thank you."

"You're welc..." he began when, abruptly, his head jerked towards the main gallery, "I hear Michel and Mr. Brown. Good luck." He hurriedly retreated to a corner of the salon behind the painting where he became almost invisible. Ellie thought he'd leave as he usually did and was trying to figure out why he'd stayed and how he'd seemed to disappear into the corner when she realized Alonzo had replaced his usually exuberant clothing with drab colors. She was still wondering why to both questions when Michel walked in, seemingly relaxed, but Ellie sensed his tension.

Shorter than Michel and entering behind him, Mr. Brown could not see the painting. Looking excited and expectant, he greeted Ellie and Cory with a smile, but when Michel moved aside, he was suddenly face-to-face with the images. Ellie saw his smile drain away and his neck get a dark red. She stood quietly as he approached the canvas. She watched to see if he scanned the painting directionally, but his eyes went immediately to the eagle and then to the snail. She saw his lips thin and could tell he was trying to think what to say. No, she corrected herself, what not to say. She was about to offer something to break the tension when, in time, she saw Michel motion her to remain quiet.

Mr. Brown's hands started shaking, then his arms and shoulders. Ellie wondered if his whole body might fly apart, and she unconsciously moved back. His emotions crowded the air until they overtook the salon and threatened to level its walls to spill out farther to flatten everyone and everything it their path.

She saw Alonzo quietly approach the painting and stand alongside it. Like a guard, thought Ellie. Her eyes grew wide. She looked from Alonzo to Michel and back to Alonzo. He thinks, both he and Michel think, Mr. Brown may try to harm it. They expected this. Michel must have called Alonzo last evening after the party. Ellie felt unable to breathe until she felt Cory's arm slip quietly around her. She felt his hand tighten around her arm and found she could breathe again. She gulped in air as Mr. Brown began.

"Everything is in the shadows. In the dark. Why is everything in the shadows?" He didn't seem to expect a response. His voice sounded menacing and too calm. "Why am I not standing front and center? I should have made that a condition of the contract." Ellie barely registered that he had taken Cory's place in the painting.

"And why," he began again and then stopped before whispering, incredulous and disbelieving, "In the sky?" He paused. "In the sky?" he repeated stretching each word out as his voice rose. "I can barely make out that it's an eagle. I should be holding it. It should be on my arm with its wings out. I should have stipulated that, too, but I trusted you." He turned to glare at Ellie.

He was now screaming. Michel didn't even try to stop him. "And where are the animals? I can only see ..." his eyes jumped from one place on the canvas to another, searching. "They should be ringed around me, my animals, there to..." He hesitated, and Ellie silently filled in the unspoken with "do my bidding." Is that what he had envisioned? He was chief potentate of an animal entourage? Is that who he thought Cory was? Horrified, Ellie was so glad she had not gone with the Santa-in-the-forest structure. Mr. Brown would have turned that into something ugly, too. With the structure she had used, he could only work with what he could see.

"And what's this on the ground? Is that the eagle's shadow by my feet?" He was now white with anger and shaking almost uncontrollably. Ellie blinked but stood up straighter. Cory dropped his arm and backed up.

Ellie stood firm as Mr. Brown's tirade continued, his voice a deafening thunder. It drenched them like a heavy cloudburst that fills the streets and pulls rising water, debris and dropped keys—trash and treasures—down into the storm drains. It increased to tsunami proportions that threatened to pull them down, too. "And, if it was here," he motioned to the painting, "I would stomp that snail." He looked at Ellie with a sneer. "What an insult." He stomped his foot for emphasis and ground his shoe into the carpet. Ellie flinched at his cruelty but remained standing tall and true. Cory looking on, not sure how he could help her, took courage from her strength and stood straighter, too.

Mr. Brown looked from one to the other of them. His body seemed to shrink into itself, his voice cracked and became hoarse, and the tirade lessened. Ellie could feel his energy begin to weaken. In a whisper that sounded to Ellie like a plea, he spat out, "What am I supposed to do with this?" He turned to Michel, who now calmly approached the canvas.

"You'll remember, Mr. Brown, that the contract stipulates you do not have to accept the painting if ... " and Michael summarized the points that pertained to the present problem.

"No," Ellie interrupted. The men all turned to her. "Please refund Mr. Brown's deposit, Michel."

"Ellie," began both Michel and Cory.

She turned to Mr. Brown. "I'm sorry the painting can't be what you hoped. I don't want your money, but the painting is still yours if you want it."

"Why would I?" he snorted. He looked at Michel. "I expect a check to be delivered this afternoon by courier," he shouted as he strode out. Alonzo quickly following him.

"Ellie, you don't have to do this," counseled Michel.

The vibrating air cleared. "It's the right thing to do, Michel." When he started on his explanation of commission contracts, Ellie broke in gently, "I mean it's what needs to happen in this particular instance for Mr. Brown. As I consider it his painting, I don't want it shown. Please store it in case he changes his mind and wants it after all."

Michel was clearly fighting his instincts. "All right," he finally agreed. "I'll do as you ask for," he thought, "three weeks. Then, I'm sending him a certified letter to say he must make a decision about whether he wants the painting or not." He put up a hand as Ellie started to protest. "Your kind offer was just that, a kind offer, not a binding agreement. After the letter is delivered, I will give him another three weeks to make his decision. And, yes, I'll send Alonzo with a check this afternoon. I still wish you had not done that, but I think I understand your motivation. I guess we'll see what happens." He shook his head sadly.

On the way home, Cory asked Ellie to help him with the little island. "Thank you, honey, I'd love to help," she replied.

Between working with Cory and extra attention from Cora, Ellie had little time to think about Mr. Brown. As she came into the kitchen early one evening, Cory met her with a picnic basket and a blanket. With a wry grin on his face, he handed her the blanket to carry.

"Like our first date," she said happily as she slipped her arm in his. He picked up the basket, and they headed to the island. They stopped at the crescent to watch the sun disappear behind the hills. The Japanese bridge glowed softly as did the matching panels on the gazebo. The butterfly bridge's lacy cables winked and sparkled. Before bringing Ellie out, Cory had lit the lanterns that bracketed the gazebo. As the sky darkened, the candles' light intensified. They walked onto an island magical with promise.

Cory spread the picnic out on a small table Ellie had tiled in a mosaic pieced together from broken china. The center medallion was a carefully cut circle that showed a small bird on a leafy branch. Not a chickadee, Ellie had explained to Connie. "I guess no one thought to make a china pattern with a chickadee." *A robin will do*, replied Connie.

"We do good work," said Ellie looking around at the twig furniture, comfortable cushions, gauzy curtains to filter the light, and the beautifully lacquered panels that could shut out the stiffest of breezes or hardest driving rain.

"That we do," agreed Cory looking around and nodding, satisfied. After they ate, he pulled an envelope from his pocket and handed it to Ellie.

"What's this?" she asked looking from the return address to Cory.

"I didn't open it, honey; it's addressed to you."

Ellie hesitated but said, "I'm being silly. Michel may be sending something completely unrelated to Mr. Brown," but she looked worried. Cory moved over to sit beside her. She read aloud.

Dear Ellie,

Mr. Brown decided he does want the painting. When he looked at it again, he seemed to receive it better and said, "Don't worry. I'm not going to destroy it. Give me at least that much credit." I'm pleasantly surprised. It only took him a week to respond to my letter asking his intent. We are working out payment.

Regards,
Michel

"Well, I'm glad for that," sighed Ellie. "I feel I can put it behind me."

"I'm glad for you." They sat awhile as the sky darkened. They left the lanterns burning as they made their way back to the house.

A month after Mr. Brown took *Journey* home, Cory and Ellie saw in the paper that he had sold his business to the conglomerate Conrad and Sons. Several weeks later, Michel called to tell Ellie a letter had been delivered to the gallery for her. Michel met her at the door and, inviting her into his office, handed her an envelope.

"The postmark is from Brazil," she observed as she opened it.

Dear Mrs. Sanborn-Waters,

My sincerest gratitude for the painting. It opened my eyes. I am out seeking what Mr. Waters has already found. You were right to place the eagle high in the sky, out of my reach ... as of yet, at least. I shouldn't have questioned your judgment, and I apologize that I was so rude to you about it. However, that is what made me realize I need to make changes, big ones.

I haven't seen a snail yet but am hoping to. A woodpecker came calling last week and has returned almost every day since. As I've seen no others, I'm claiming it as mine. Don't tell me what it means, I want to learn about it for myself.

Again, in gratitude,

Clarence Brown

After she'd read the note, Michel handed her a check. "I didn't say or suggest anything to him. In a letter to me, he stated this is what he wants to pay you for the painting."

Ellie's jaw dropped. "Michel, it's twice what he originally agreed upon."

"It's yours. Your instincts paid off. Here's your reward."

"That's not why I let him have the painting," she said shaking her head sadly.

He looked at her a moment. "True," he agreed. "Then let me use the word blessing instead of reward."

CHAPTER 20

Ellie was sitting on the bench they had recently found at an artist's colony and had given themselves for their third anniversary present. It fit perfectly between the two young maple trees and had the best view of the bee garden. The plants had grown well in the last four years. The bushes, with small boulders interspersed among them, formed a loose hedge at the back of the garden. The bushes had matured enough to start filling in and intertwine their branches over and around the boulders. The dozen trees they had planted were well above Cory's head now. The remains of spring blossoms had strewn themselves about their bases and had scattered onto the flagstones in the seating area by the maples.

Ellie smiled as she thought, "It's like pink snow flakes. I couldn't have created a more perfect painting than what I'm seeing." She drank it in to memorize it for future use.

Cory arrived with a tray of coffee and cookies. "Thank you, honey," said Ellie as he placed the tray on the nearby table and handed her a cup.

He turned to get his cup but left it on the tray as several bees flew in. He and Ellie had been waiting a long time for the hive to come back this year. He knew ordinary bees do not keep multiple dwellings, and they had wondered over the last several weeks if Zanzibar would bring them back this year. Every spring he wondered, but for the last three years, they had moved back in before Easter. The weather had warmed early this year, but the bees had not returned until now just a couple of weeks before solstice.

"Hello," said Cory to them as they walked around on his hand and arm before flitting off.

"Ploppers?"

"Yup, all of them."

"I've been watching them move back in and thinking about the last three years, four, really."

He sat down next to her. "They've been wonderful years. Happy anniversary."

"Yes, they have; happy anniversary." They sat in companionable stillness for a few minutes. Ellie sensed Cory had something on his mind and said softly, "The trees have certainly grown up well. I remember planting them in the first few months after we met." She smiled into his eyes and slipped her hand into his.

He squeezed her hand gently as he nodded thoughtfully. "That was such a magical time." He looked lovingly at her, "and the magic has simply continued." He sipped his coffee and breathed in the warm, scented air.

She tried again, "I hope some butterflies find the island soon."

"Me, too."

Ellie was sure he had something to say. She wasn't sure though if she should let him think it out or coax him to tell her. "What is it, Cory?" she finally asked as she leaned her head on his shoulder.

"I think there's a trip coming up," he said finally.

They took lots of trips, and it took Ellie a moment to realize he wasn't talking about an art show or a speaking engagement. "Ahh," she said looking up at him. "And you're wondering if I'm coming along?"

"Yes. I've never been responsible for taking someone with me."

Ellie frowned slightly. "If I'm to go, aren't I responsible for myself?" Cory looked at her with a raised eyebrow. Ellie continued encouragingly, "Would I be sent if I couldn't handle it?"

"I hadn't thought of it that way." She could feel his shoulder relaxing.

"Honey, have you been worrying about doing the whole thing for both of us?"

She sat up when Cory shrugged. "You take such good care of me," she said rubbing his hand.

He nodded and let out his breath as if he'd been holding it. "I think we'll be going as soon as the bees finish moving back."

"Do you know where we're going?" Cory nodded. "Where?" she asked.

"To the old forest." Ellie blinked. She hadn't expected that.

"Wow," she whispered. "Have you ever been there?"

Cory shook his head. Knowing he'd always feel protective of Ellie, he put an arm around her and said, "It's almost summer, and travel should be easy, but we need to check what we have for hiking and sleeping out."

"You think we're going to be gone long?" asked Ellie beginning to grasp the possible scope of the trip.

"Even if it's just for one or two days, we need to be prepared."

"Of course. You're right." She paused and then asked, "Can we sit here a bit longer and enjoy everything?"

"Sure. I don't think we're leaving in the next hour. Have you looked at our upcoming commitment schedule though?"

"No," she offered tentatively. Cory pulled it up on his phone. "Oh, there is nothing on it for two weeks. I see why you've been wondering about this trip." Cory nodded. They sat watching bees flit back and forth.

"I think I'd like to get busy organizing," Ellie said abruptly. "Are you finished with your coffee?" Cory handed her his cup. She gathered napkins, plates and cups quickly, clattering them together in her haste. Loading everything onto the tray, she hurried back to the house.

Cory sighed. This is not how he'd wanted her to react. This is why he'd waited to say anything. He had wanted to be careful how he presented the upcoming trip. He thought now about what he could have done differently and shook his head. He didn't know what else he could have done.

He was reminded of the first few times he'd been sent. I was just as nervous, he reminded himself, but I had Connie. He looked up into the trees. He was surprised she hadn't shown up yet. She always heralded a trip. Now, that is odd, he thought and followed Ellie back to the house. He was almost to the break between the bee garden and the yard when he saw her sitting on the bottom porch step. He thought, at first, she was crying with her head in her hands. He was about to run over to her when he saw she was bent over petting Cora. He quietly backed up. Cora had better medicine than he could offer.

He decided to walk to the Japanese bridge. Maybe Connie was there. He stopped, not even feeling like going to the bridge. I'm never this unsettled, thought Cory. What is wrong with me? I never have bad moods like this. He tried to shake off his feelings of confusion and indecisiveness. Maybe I could take a quick trip to the edge of the desert and take Ralph some cheese. He looked at his phone. No, I don't think I want to start this late. I could take the rowboat out onto the lake or just go to the island for a bit. That wouldn't take as long. Maybe Ellie would like to come. That had possibilities until he remembered Ellie wanted to start organizing, and Cora was with her. He didn't want to intrude.

He felt drained of ambition and, when a bamboo leaf brushed his face, he found he was wandering down the path to the spring. Realizing he was more than halfway there, he decided he might as well go on. Too absorbed in his melancholy to enjoy what was around him, he failed to notice the dark mass in the sky. It was coming up quickly from behind and gaining on him. He felt the disturbance of air before he heard the feathers.

As a large hawk landed in front of him, Cory gasped. He had never been this close to such a large bird and wasn't sure what to do. He realized it was one of his and would not harm him, but its beak and talons looked awfully big and as sharp as meat hooks. The bird stood looking at him. *Really? You don't know me? Get it together, Cory.* Suddenly, Cory, said reverently, "Of course. You're Berkeley. I'm so glad to meet you finally. I've heard you so many times." He looked the bird over with awe. He didn't know what type of hawk Berkeley was and wished for the bird book he had had as a kid. "Which reminds me," he said. "Is Connie coming?" Berkeley eyed him a moment longer, pivoted and starting walking to the spring. They were less than six feet away, so flying would be kind of silly, but still, thought Cory, I don't think I ever thought of a hawk walking anywhere.

Berkeley stepped sedately around to the right of the spring. Cory was about to say, "The path actually goes to the left," when he thought, a person probably doesn't tell his totem hawk anything. So, he followed Berkeley around to where he knew there was nothing. Except, he now saw a small pool. He searched his memory for indications of one. No, there had never been anything there. As keeper of the estate, Cory checked the spring every few months to make sure everything was as it should be. He and Ellie had walked the grounds after the last snow melted in April. One of them would have noticed a pool there or even just that one was forming.

Cory took out his phone to take notes. He judged the size to be no larger than four feet back to front and about five feet wide. He couldn't tell how deep it was. Though clear, the water was a luminous azure like the famous pool in Yellowstone. Well, almost like the other pool because this one seemed to give off an emerald and aquamarine mist that sparkled on the water's surface and rose as a fine spray to hang in the air above it. Either the colors or the sparkles made it impossible for him to fathom the depth.

He slowly became aware that Berkeley was standing beside him. "Is it real?" he asked the bird. *What do you think?* "I think it is." *Then, it is.* "But, how does that work that it is because I think it?" asked Cory. Berkeley turned to him. *Look past your illusions.* Cory's shoulders sagged. "After everyone I've guided, I can't believe I forgot," he whispered in disbelief.

Berkeley continued looking at him. Cory came back from his thoughts and turned to the hawk. He had seen that look on Connie. "We'll leave in the morning." Berkeley planted his talons in the grass. "All right," said Cory with resolve, "We'll leave this afternoon." Seemingly satisfied with Cory's response, Berkeley stretched his wings to depart. Cory moved back to let him have the necessary room. As he watched him wheel away, Cory could hear his cry. He quickly made his way back to the house. He found Ellie in the bedroom with clothes laid out.

"I heard the hawk. Cora explained what it meant." She nodded to the window sill where Cora was sunning herself.

She had fallen asleep still holding part of the strawberry Ellie had given her. Cory described his experience at the spring. Ellie was shaking her head. At first, Cory thought she had changed her mind and was refusing to go, or maybe it was just that she didn't believe him, but she said, "That was not there in April. Of course, we go now."

"You sure?"

She came over and put her arms around his waist. "I think if your hawk comes to visit, you just say, 'Yes, sir. What do you want me to do?' I don't think you mess around." Cory had to smile. Ellie always had a way of putting things in perspective for him. She released him and turned back to the bed. "I've made piles of things I think we might need. I'm not sure what we put it all in though."

Cory looked through everything. "All good choices, but there's too much. We don't want to carry heavy packs. One change of clothing, the lined jackets with hoods, extra socks, boots, jeans. My pouch and your sketch pad and pencils. I think that's all we can do. We'll hook water bottles onto our belt loops and take a small sack of food."

Ellie had started looking worried. No, Cory amended. She looked scared. "Ellie, honey, we'll be on the estate the whole time. It's not like a trip to, I don't know, the Idaho forests. We'll be taken care of. It's a pilgrimage and a learning. It's a time for beginning the transition into something new, who we need to grow into next. We'll be provided for. We just need to take some things to make rough ground and possible rain easier to deal with, and some food in case we get caught out. That's all. It's okay. Really."

"That's what Cora said, but it's not what I'm used to. My dad used to plan every detail of a vacation, and it all feels so odd, but you've done this before, so, okay." She sighed and turned to Cory. "All right. We have the piles. What do we put it all in?"

"Ahh, Madam," said Cory, assuming a magician's tone. "I will show you a great wonder!" He went to his study, rummaged noisily in the closet, and came back with two bags. They weren't quite satchels, nor were they quite backpacks. "Voila! My own invention."

"Uh, I remember that line from *Through the Looking Glass*. That guy's inventions didn't work so well. What's to make me think yours will?" she challenged like the magic show's skeptic.

"Humph," was all Cory could think of as a response and showed Ellie how they worked. "They are lighter than backpacks and easy to carry, but they have a lot of room." Ellie still looked skeptical. "I've used them on almost all my trips. This bag went through the desert with me. This one I made for day trips, but I think it's a good size for you."

"Okay," she finally relented. "Let's pack, shower, and eat something so we can start."

CHAPTER 21

With the season approaching solstice, most of their evening walk was in the light. Ellie was interested in everything, but Cory noticed she seemed unsettled. Usually so calm, her mood was again affecting him. He wondered what he should say. He was struggling to word what he said carefully. He didn't want a repeat of Ellie's reaction this afternoon. Abruptly, he realized he should simply say what he felt he needed to. That was the only thing respectful to Ellie. Trying to tiptoe around her only separated them. They'd been together almost four years and knew each other well. He just needed to be honest. It was as if he'd suddenly forgotten how. That was silly. They talked together all the time.

He cleared his throat. "I don't know why we both seem to be so antsy. We're usually not like this." Ellie looked at him, a bit defensively, he thought. "Ellie? Am I right?"

"Yah," she finally admitted sighing and biting her lip. He linked his arm in hers. Though their strides were similar, they slowed their pace and matched their steps. "Maybe it's because I've never done this. I felt something was up. I mean with me and with you and with, well, everything. By that, I mean I could feel it around me when I'd go sketch and even when I was doing stuff around the house or at the gallery, and even when I was talking to people, say, on the sidewalk. It's a bit frightening, well, not frightening, just a bit confusing and uncomfortable, I guess, would be the words. It felt as if the universe was saying, 'Listen; pay attention,' and I didn't know what I was supposed to pay attention to." She ran out of steam and became quiet, but before Cory thought of a response, she added, "And you weren't your calm, assured self, and that did scare me."

"Oh, honey, I'm so sorry. I should have said something before today." Cory pulled her close. "I didn't notice it at first. I guess I was too busy thinking about what else needs to be done for the butterfly garden and kept thinking I was just too involved in the details. When I finally realized what was going on, it was almost today, and then everything happened so fast, and ... " he paused and looked around, "and here we are. It's also been so long since I was sent I kind of forgot what it feels like."

"Does it always feel like this?" asked Ellie both curious and wanting reassurance.

Cory sighed and said, "No. I have to admit I haven't been this unsettled since my first couple of trips. I thought it was because I'd have you along and was hoping it would be an easy trip for your first one, but I'm beginning to realize ..." he stopped. "No, I knew. I just kept trying to tell myself I was wrong."

"Wrong about what, my dearest?" Ellie asked softly when he didn't continue.

"I've gotten little signs for a number of weeks now that we'd be heading to the wild. It won't be an easy trip." He was about to offer Ellie reassurance when she looked deep into his eyes, stood up straight and planted herself in front of him.

"It will be what it needs to be. I could say, 'Don't you think it might turn out to be easier like your desert trip was?' but it needs to be what it is. You've taught me that. If it's not what it's supposed to be, we just have to do it all again at some point. As you would say, 'God and our angels won't leave us to flounder on our own.' As I would say, 'The universe has our back.'"

Cory put down his bag and hugged her tightly to him, more for himself than for her. "You give me such strength," he said kissing her hair. "Onward, we go."

They both could feel the change. The evening seemed more friendly; they felt calmer. "I can feel hopefulness," remarked Ellie. Cory nodded. The sky began to darken. Cory was looking at it and trying to gauge if they could comfortably sleep out when he heard a soft whir of wings and turned. Ellie already had her arm out. Connie lit and hopped happily around on Ellie's sleeve. "Connie, dear, where have you been? We thought surely you would have been around today." *I had to get ready.*

"Ready for what, Gertrude Trudy Daisy Dais Daisychain?" asked Cory using all her pet names. *The trip. I'm going with you.* "You are? That's great, Dais!" Cory had started feeling better after he and Ellie talked. Now, he was almost elated. A palpable sense of relief flowed through him.

"Oh, I'm so glad," said Ellie. Connie preened her feathers.

Abruptly, she was all business. *You need shelter for tonight. It's going to rain.* "It's not supposed to," Cory began, "but I know better than to contradict you, Dais. We'll follow."

Connie flew ahead, seemingly scouting out a shelter or maybe just to get a better view of what she was looking for. "I feel better already," said Ellie. "We're starting out really well. I feel pretty silly for being scared earlier."

Cory thought about not saying anything but then decided he should. "I was scared, too. It's okay. In fact, if you are scared, or worried, or angry, or anything like that, it's much better to acknowledge it and release it than to try to get through it by yourself. Connie taught me that, but I forgot." He stopped and had Ellie stop, too. "It may be a lesson we'll need to remember in the coming days."

"You're getting so serious again. You really think it's going to be tough?"

"I have never been called on a trip and felt what I have been feeling: the sheer weight of importance of what we are undertaking. I've always gone out and explored and learned through my experiences as they happened and then kept learning afterwards as I put experiences together into larger contexts. I imagine it's like you making a bunch of small sketches and then redrawing them into one, huge composite piece."

Ellie was startled. "I've never done that; I've never even thought of doing that. What a great challenge."

"What do you mean? I see you do it all the time," said Cory.

"Oh, I take parts of one sketch and incorporate them into other pieces, but to take a multitude of small bits and pieces and make a sort of collage of them so they make one whole? I have never done that. Maybe that's why I was invited on this trip." A thought hit Ellie at the same time it did Cory, or maybe it bounced from one to the other. "I think our experiences and responses to them are going to be very different for each of us," she said sucking her cheeks in and pursing her mouth.

"I think so, too," said Cory. "I think we're going to need to tell each other more than we usually do. Maybe we've gone along for so long now mostly seeing things in the same way that we've forgotten how to share the differences that make us who we are."

Ellie nodded thoughtfully. "I agree. They make us who we are individually and as a team." She was quiet a moment before adding, "I just hope we don't have to do any of this alone. I don't mean without Connie. I mean you and me, separately."

Cory felt his blood turn icy. He could sense the truth in what she had just said. His eyes started smarting as he said, "We might, sweetheart. I don't know, but it feels as if we might."

Ellie looked up at him. "I think so, too. I was hoping I was wrong, but I think we might. Hopefully, it will be little experiences like part of an afternoon if I sketch, say, and you, I don't know, collect berries on a nearby hillside." Her voice trailed off, "I hope it's not overnight," but Cory heard what she said.

"We'll face whatever when it arrives. That's all we can do."

"At least, I don't think it will be tonight."

"I don't either, but Connie was right," said Cory as the first spits of rain reached them. They were still walking through the foothills though the land had started to rise. Ahead, they could clearly see the line of trees that marked the forest's boundary. This was young forest, but it offered plenty of protection. Connie circled in but immediately looped back. Cory and Ellie began to jog, partly to keep her in sight, but also because they could now see lightning.

Cory yelled, "Run for it," as a large clap of thunder shook the ground. They crossed the first line of trees as rain began to pelt them. A strong wind had sprung up and was driving the rain behind them. Connie circled back in and then darted between several trees. They saw the cabin she was heading to and made a dash for it. Cory forced the door closed behind them as wind and rain hammered the exterior.

"Where's Connie?" asked Ellie as she searched the nooks and corners.

"She's on the mantle; she's okay," he said.

Ellie put her bag down and went over to her. "You okay, Trudy dear?" she asked feeling her feathers. They were mostly dry, but Ellie could feel her little heart quickly thumping. "Thank you for finding the cabin."

Cory was opening doors and drawers. He found candles and lit several and placed them around the room. "We'll be safe and dry here," he said. "There's even a water pump and access to a, well, an attached outhouse, I guess you'd say."

Ellie came over to see and smiled wryly. "I've camped," she said. "Not in a long time, but I'll manage." Cory showed her the water he'd collected from the hand pump. Ellie looked around at the fireplace. "We can make a fire in the morning and have hot water. It's all good, an adventure."

"We have enough wood. I'm going to make a fire now to dry our clothes." Cory squatted in front of the fireplace and laid logs and kindling. He lit a small pine branch and got it burning before stuffing it under the kindling.

"I'm wetter than I thought, but that will get everything dry," Ellie said as she pulled a chair in front of the fire and laid her jacket on it. She took Cory's from him and laid it over the chair's seat. Surveying the room, Ellie wished she had a camera. "I so want to capture the feel of this place and the light with the candles." She pulled her sketch pad and pencil case out of her bag. "I want to make a couple of sketches before bed," she said as she walked around to find the best angle. Cory helped her carry a bench to a far corner, and soon, she was absorbed in her drawing.

It's as if she enters the paper, thought Cory watching her work. He looked for Connie and found her in a warm nook of the chimney with her head under her wing. I guess I'm the only one feeling fidgety. I usually have a plan by this time in a trip. Truthfully, I've always had some kind of plan even before starting out. He thought about previous trips.

He smiled as he remembered his first one. He had been all of 16, and his parents had allowed him to go camping by himself for one night. I was so excited. He smiled and felt again the newness of that first trip. Connie had to teach me everything. Mom made sure I had practical things. Connie ensured I had spiritual things. It was midsummer, so I didn't need to building any fires. In fact, Mom forbade it. Cory chuckled as he remembered her scolding, "and next thing, I'll be getting a call from the police that you're in the hospital and the woods are burning up."

"I promise I won't burn anything down," he had said as he kissed her goodbye.

With a start, he counted back to the last time he had seen her; it had been several months. When he and Ellie got back, they needed to make time to see both their families.

He thought again about this trip and how different it felt than previous ones. On that first trip, he hadn't even taken his remembrance pouch. He had just made it and had put it safely away in a drawer. Connie had tried to get him to take it, but he didn't want to get it dirty. He was still too pleased with it. Shaking his head, Cory laughed softly to himself, "That was perhaps the most important lesson I learned on that trip. Mementos of my life aren't meant for admiration. They're meant to be used, and they grow more precious as they become more worn from use." He chuckled and added, "Kind of like Hank."

You were my first animal friend, Hank. By the time I laid you to rest, one of your front legs was loose, you'd lost most of your mane, and part of your stuffing was gone. I stitched your leg back on and looked you in your one remaining eye and said goodbye and thank you for the many good years you were my friend and companion.

Cory had wrapped Hank in a ceremonial towel—an old towel but one he washed and scented with rosemary for remembrance. He made a funeral pyre in the fire pit. His mother had not been happy about that, but his dad said to let him be, he was just being Cory, and they could have it a lot worse like some of their friends did with their teenagers.

Hank's other eye and a sprig of rosemary were the first objects that went into Cory's pouch. It was kind of creepy now when he came across that plastic eye, but his intentions had been noble and he had been, what, 15? Leave it to a teenager.

Cory came back to the present and the uncertainties of this trip. It still bothered him that he was unsure about everything, that he had nothing he could count on. He blushed suddenly and felt ashamed. "I'm so sorry," he whispered. "I have Ellie and Connie. Neither of them seems concerned. Most importantly, I have You. I'm ready," he added aloud.

"What's that?" asked Ellie looking up and smiling at him. She was putting her things back in her bag. Cory helped her move the bench back and said, "I have to quit worrying. It's a slap in God's face, and it does nothing productive."

"Very true," Ellie said gently. "We just need to feel and follow. So, where do we sleep? On the floor?"

"Yup." They decided to put the blanket under them for padding as the cabin was warm and their jackets were now dry. Cory added another log and banked the fire. They traded their now warm, dry jackets with their damp jeans. Ellie made pillows out of their extra clothes and blew out the candles. Rain and wind steadily pelted the windows and roof. Thunder rolled above them, but they slept soundly.

CHAPTER 22

They awoke to complete quiet. The rain had stopped, and the wind had exhausted itself and moved on. "I've never heard nothing," Ellie said, her voice sounding too loud. She lowered it and continued, "It's as if we're in a, what are those vacuum things called?"

"Deprivation chamber, but I feel anything but deprived," Cory replied softly.

She nodded. "I hate to break the mood. It feels as if it will shatter if we get up and go about our usual morning's business, but we can't just stay here forever." They got up and stretched, surprised they weren't more sore or stiff after sleeping on the floor. Cory stirred the fire and heated water for washing.

Ellie found Connie. Letting her out, Ellie could feel the softness of air scrubbed clean of lingering dust. The sun was just starting to stretch fingers in among the trees, and the morning glistened after its bath. "Oh, Cory," she called back into the cabin, "it's a gorgeous morning."

He came to see. After a moment, he sniffed and said, "It smells good, too." They left the door open as they ate part of the food they had brought. Cory tamped out the remaining embers. Ellie had already started out the door when Cory stopped her. "I always say a 'Thank you' to whatever and whomever has helped me on a trip."

"Of course," said Ellie. "I'm sorry." She joined Cory in thanking the cabin, the wind and rain, their animals and the world of spirit, and they started out.

As they walked, they talked about the last four years, their future, the new animals. Ellie wanted to pick up every rock, leaf, and acorn that caught her attention. "You won't have room for everything," laughed Cory and instructed her on how to find things that represent the essence of an entire experience.

When he finished his lecture, she said brightly, "Like a Gestalt," and proceeded to educate Cory about wholes that are bigger than the sums of their parts.

"I just realized ... "

"What?" asked Ellie when he didn't continue.

"That describes how I feel about the bridges, how they seem to be more than just two separate bridges."

"Yes, they interact symbolically to help us feel and think in different ways."

"That's really cool," said Cory thoughtfully. "That has possibilities for how I talk about them when I'm giving a tour. Um, back to mementos," he added gently, "You maybe don't need to collect remembrances, at least not like I do."

"What do you mean?"

"Everybody likes to have reminders of favorite things, you know, like taking photos on a vacation or buying souvenirs, but to collect mementos of where you are—uh, not a place, I mean a way you are at a certain time in your life—is something not everyone needs to do. You might be meant to do something different than that."

"Oh, I see," Ellie began and then added, "but I have animals, well, an animal, like you do."

"True. We all have teachers. They just can be different depending on who we are and where we are on our particular journeys. That's all." He looked at Ellie and smiled. "Just don't do what I do just because I do it. Something else may be what you're supposed to do." She nodded.

They chatted companionably as they strolled easily over the mulched forest floor. Finding blackberry bushes in a sunny clearing, they gathered what they could fit in the small tub Cory had packed for that purpose. "We can eat off the land for a good part of our meals," he said as he carefully gleaned the berries and tried to stay clear of the thorns.

At the last minute, Ellie had packed her artist's gloves, fingerless and made from supple leather, and was working much more quickly. "I need a pair of those," considered Cory.

"I'm glad I brought them, but they're getting juice stains," she complained.

"How's that different from the paint that's already on them?" asked Cory.

"I don't know," she responded laughing. "Somehow, it just seems to be."

"Maybe the berries are suggesting that you try natural dyes," he teased.

"Oh, funny man; funny, funny man," she retorted. They chatted and teased, and the day was bright. It felt like a day for going to ... Cory paled as the memory of his first fiancée and the carousel ride and the aftermath enveloped him almost jarring him off his feet. He pushed the painful thoughts away. He didn't want to tell Ellie. The day had been so nice up until this happened. He hadn't thought of that woman or that day since his trip through the desert with Ralph. Why was he thinking of her now?

"Cory?" Ellie had stopped and was looking at him. He finally met her eyes. "I thought we were going to share, no matter what the experience is we're having."

"I don't … okay, you're right … yah, we did." He sighed and told her what had just happened.

"Oh, honey," she said and put her arms around him, berry-stains and all. "I'm not going anywhere."

"I know you're not. I just feel like I'm losing something important, but I don't know what it is. I feel I should do something to stop it from happening."

Ellie felt her thoughts and then tried to put into words what she knew to be true, "If you lose something, even if it is really important, then it's meant to be lost. What if you lost Connie?"

"I'd cry," said Cory. "A lot! If it was just that I hadn't seen her and couldn't feel her, I'd want to go look for her, but I'd know whatever happened was what needed to. It doesn't mean I'd have to like it," he finished up stubbornly.

"But you would," reasoned Ellie, not even sure how she knew this. "You'd have to accept and be grateful and go on joyfully." Cory was still looking stubborn. "You'd mourn. Of course, you would. You'd be worried, but you know Connie can look after herself better than either one of us can look after ourselves. Most of all, you know to whom we all belong. You, better than most people, understand the consequences of not accepting or of not working through something to acceptance."

Cory stared at her, blinked, started smiling and then laughing. He hugged Ellie to him and then picked her up and whirled her in a circle. After he set her back down, he said, "You always find the balance. You always make things better. I don't have to be in control of everything. In fact, it's better if

I'm not. Maybe this is one of the things I'm supposed to learn on this trip."

"What is that?" asked Ellie.

"Deeper trust in the divine, in the infinite, in everything being the way it's supposed to be even if I don't like it." He let out his breath. "Now, I wouldn't mind finding a remembrance."

"How about this?" Bending down, Ellie picked up something Cory couldn't see and handed him a small, lumpy pebble the size and color of a ripe blackberry.

"You do understand mementos," said Cory putting it in his pouch. "We've filled the tub. We need to leave the rest for the animals."

"And fairies," said Ellie.

"And the fairies," replied Cory indulgently.

"No, I'm serious. Woodland spirits use blackberries, too."

"I apologize," said Cory seriously. "How do you know about woodland spirits?"

"I'm an artist," she said as if this explained it.

They gathered their jackets and bags. Cory pointed a direction, and they started out again. Connie had flown off earlier that morning. They knew she could find them when and where she needed to. Cory figured they would not enter the old-growth forest until late the next morning at the earliest. Walking in the young forest was easy, and they looked around as they walked and pointed out birds and animals to each other. Even with the trees in full leaf, sun filtered through the canopy and warmed them. The forest was dotted with small clearings in which they rested. As the day progressed and the sun began to get too warm, they stayed in the dappled shade under the trees.

"I don't know why I was worried yesterday," remarked Ellie as she watched two squirrels chasing each other. "The cabin was fine last night. It was kind of fun not knowing where I'd be sleeping."

"I'm missing something here," said Cory. "You said yesterday that your family camped."

"We camped, but my dad always made reservations. He'd say something like, 'We have to make it to Granite City this evening. We have reservations at the campground.' Did your family just take off, no plan?"

"Oh, my parents always had a plan, but sometimes the plans were very, uh, 'loose' might be the word. My dad liked camping anywhere but an organized campground, so I hardly ever knew where we'd be any particular night. It was a lot of fun. Maybe not all that comfortable some nights, but always an adventure."

By afternoon, the forest floor, which had been smooth and level, turned hilly and rough. Cory showed Ellie how to step down with one foot planted sideways to better keep her balance. They found themselves on a path too narrow to walk side by side. It grew steeper the farther they went. With the ground sloping and the sometimes slippery mulch underfoot, they slowed their pace and used their hands to either pull themselves up inclines or to hold themselves steady as they descended. Finally, the path leveled off. Able to relax and not have to put all their concentration on their feet, they stopped. With a sigh, Ellie lowered herself onto a fallen log and rubbed her calves. Cory set his bag down and stretched his shoulders.

"That was a bit of a trek," remarked Ellie.

"Yah, I wasn't expecting that today," replied Cory as he looked back at where they'd come from: at the young trees and patches of wildflowers poking up around them, the sunny spots and dappled shade, the soft colors and sounds of birds.

Ellie joined him. "I'd love to come back when I have the time to spend a few days just to paint. It's magical in here: the juxtapositions of light and shadow, of colors, of canopy and openness. It's lovely."

"It is," replied Cory nodding. "Ready?"

"Yes." They turned and walked up a small knoll to see where they were going and froze. Up ahead was a sunny meadow. But beyond it, like an eclipse, loomed the dense, dark growth that signaled entry into the old forest.

CHAPTER 23

Ellie's face turned chalky. "I thought we were a day out," she said quietly, but she had started trembling.

"I did, too," said Cory swallowing hard. He looked up into the sky.

"I'm not ready. I'm just not ready." Ellie kept whispering.

"It'll be okay," Cory comforted. "At least it's only the middle of the afternoon. We have plenty of daylight."

Ellie wheeled around to face him. "Daylight to do what?" she asked. Cory was about to answer when she went on, "To get somewhere specific? Where? To do … what do we do? Wander around?" He realized she was almost hysterical. "I don't understand. I thought you always had a guide. There's no Ralph, no Zanzibar. No Connie, even. I don't want to do this." She started crying and sank to the ground with a thud. Cory was stunned. He'd never seen her like this. Then, he heard her say, "Oh, please, no!"

"Sweetie, sweetie, it's okay." Cory tore his bag off his shoulders and knelt beside her. Laying her head on his chest, he rocked her and stroked her hair. He could feel her shaking.

"I'm scared," she sobbed. "I thought I was over it, but the feeling's back."

Cory had to admit that, up close, the face of the old forest was intimidating. "It's just that those huge, old trees look daunting," he said.

"No," said Ellie pulling away and looking at him. "That's not it. What way are we going to go?"

It seemed to Cory that she knew the answer. He frowned and looked at the trees. "Once we enter, we're going to head west."

He thought she was going to start crying again. Instead, she took his face in her hands. "No, baby, you're heading west. I have to head east," she said as she rubbed her thumbs across his cheeks. Cory sat stunned.

Suddenly, he leaped up and, having to get rid of extra energy, kicked a nearby boulder. He quickly stopped. He had to get himself under control if not for himself, at least, for Ellie. "I know; I know," he said trying to calm himself. "I can feel it, too. I didn't think it would happen this fast. I don't like this at all."

In the face of Cory's anger and dismay, Ellie was appalled, and her eyes grew large, but as a breeze started up, she began to find her calm center. Presently, she said, "You're right. It will be okay. Somehow. Cory?" she called softly. He came back and sat down by her.

"I couldn't take losing you." His voice came out a strangled sob.

"It's not me you're losing. I'm not getting that sense at all. I think we're being separated temporarily for a larger purpose. I really feel it's just for one night. I hoped earlier that by saying something about an afternoon and drawing and berry picking, I could change how or when it would happen. I should know better by now. The choices aren't up to me."

They both sat quietly. Cory reached for Ellie's hand, which she placed in his. The breeze intensified and ruffled their hair, cooled Cory's overheated face, and dried Ellie's tears. As they sat and let the spirits of the young forest and old forest talk to them, they began to relax. Their thoughts and emotions cleared, and they were able to accept. "I still don't understand why," offered Cory, "but I understand that it's important to do, and that it's okay."

"Me, too," said Ellie finally. "It is okay. Not the helper I expected though," she remarked with a shrug and a laugh.

"Not what helper?" asked Cory, confused.

"The wind." She looked at him as she asked, "Have you ever had a non-animal teacher?"

"No, I haven't," he said slowly. He thought some more. "Actually, I guess I have. I just never thought of them being like my animals."

"When I was a little girl, the wind used to talk to me like it did just now."

"Really?"

Ellie was nodding as she said, "I had completely forgotten until this happened." She looked at Cory and stroked his face as she said, "I guess we can't say we'll meet at a particular place tomorrow, can we? But, I know without doubt I will see you by noon," she nodded to the old forest, "somewhere in there."

"This is a hard, hard lesson," sighed Cory, his eyes moist.

He ate some of the berries and made Ellie take the rest and most of the other food. He wanted to give her the blanket, too. "It's too bulky for me to carry with everything else," she said. "You keep it."

She kissed him and started across the meadow towards the old forest as Cora came skipping up. Ellie turned to show Cory. He already had his arm raised to shield his eyes. She thought he didn't see, so she called out, "Cora is here."

She saw him nod. A few moments later she thought she heard him say, "Connie just flew in."

Everything is as it should be, called the wind to them both.

CHAPTER 24

With her mind now cleared from doubt and the anxiety of anticipation, Ellie found herself beginning to look forward to her adventure. Besides, she had Cora with her now. She turned and saw Cory still standing there, watching her progress. Always my protector, she thought fondly and waved.

After seeing Cory start on his path, she turned and approached a small boulder that was half way across the meadow. She clambered up it. Cora scurried in the nearby grass until she was tired. She came and sat by Ellie and looked hopeful until Ellie handed her a blackberry. After eating a few berries herself, Ellie decided she wasn't as hungry as she had thought. Cora had not finished the one she'd been given, so Ellie put the rest away and got out her pencils and pad. She turned to sketch the scene behind her, but her pencil remained poised above the paper. The meadow had turned golden, and the young forest shimmered in the afternoon light. She scanned the meadow but didn't see Cory and assumed he had already entered the old forest at a different point.

She sat looking and memorizing, considering how to capture the light, but she waited too long. The light faded. The golden glow disappeared. Thinking clouds were rolling in, she looked up, but the sky was still the brilliant blue it had been all day. I can at least make a picture of the way the day is now, she thought. Turning to her paper, she was confused to see an entire sketch—the meadow, the young forest, Cory walking towards her, and Connie flying above him. "I don't understand," she whispered. She quietly closed the pad and put everything away before rousing Cora.

*   *   *

Cory watched Ellie leave, his eyes shaded from the glare. He saw her cross the meadow and disappear into the duskiness of the old forest. He was glad Cora was with her. When she had called back to tell him that, he had scanned the sky for Connie. Even with shading his eyes from the brightness, he felt blinded. He stood waiting, thinking she might fly in. He felt more alone than he had in many years. He wondered what he would do if, IF, he repeated, he couldn't find Ellie tomorrow or the next day or ever. Stop it, he scolded. That isn't helpful. Is that what you feel? No. He had to admit he felt hopeful. He felt she was right; they'd meet up by noon tomorrow. "Why so sad then, Cory?" he asked himself.

"Right," he answered. "Do what you know to do, what you've always done." He picked up his bag, slung it over his shoulders, and started towards the old forest. He chose a route that would bring him into the forest farther west. The terrain looked rougher and the meadow grass taller than the path Ellie had chosen, but as he was alone, it didn't matter. He was used to hiking.

As he walked, he took stock of where he'd been. He pictured the estate now with its bee garden and the butterfly garden that was almost ready. He counted the new animals. He was especially fond of the young kangaroo, the joey, that had shown up last fall, and the bullfrog that had taken up residence near his rowboat a year or so ago. He thought about the lecture series Ellie had encouraged him to offer, and the tours he gave, her art shows, the book they were working on together. Together. He liked that word and the comfort it offered. Together with Ellie, with Connie and all his other animals, with … well, with just everything.

"Together with everything." He spoke it aloud as he reflected on his life, which still had the power to amaze him. So many wonderful blessings in the last four years since Ellie's arrival. He said a short thank you and then made a longer apology when he realized that the last time he had counted his life had been just before Connie had led Ellie to the estate. "I've been remiss," he said. "I am so sorry. I've been following the calling, the life work You set for me, but that's no excuse not to stop and remember."

"Oh," he exclaimed as his face fell. He stopped walking and sighed. "I know I can't prevent it or speed things up, but please help me find it quickly." He looked up at the sun, which was still high in the sky. Even so, Cory began to hurry. As he crossed the tree line, it was as if the sun was abruptly snuffed out.

*　　*　　*

"I thought it would be darker in here," Ellie remarked to Cora, who was riding in her jacket pocket. "The trees are so tall and densely packed I thought I'd already need a candle." Dividing the candles had been easy when she and Cory parted earlier. Dividing up their one box of matches had proved more difficult. Finally, Cory had torn off one of the striking surfaces, and putting it in one of his jacket pockets, he dropped matches in the other. He then gave the rest and the waterproof case to Ellie.

"I'm glad you are with me, Cora," she continued, "and I'm even more glad Connie is with Cory." She started to say something else because it felt good to talk to someone, but she felt nudged to be quiet. She looked down. Cora had fallen asleep, anyway. Ellie breathed in the moist, leafy aroma of the plants and the spicy fragrance of the pines. Unlike the young forest, which was mostly birches and other hard woods, the old forest was almost all evergreens: pine, fur, laurel, holly.

Ellie was content to wander and take in whatever presented itself. She wondered about her earlier mood when she had panicked and said this was exactly what she didn't want to do. It was as if she had had to say that to decide if she meant it. To test it. That was it. To test what it sounded like to hear myself say it, and then decide how I felt about it, and whether I meant it at all. Emotional outbursts are so unlike me, she thought. Poor Cory. I probably freaked him out.

She wasn't wearing a watch, and she hadn't brought her phone. Looking up into the canopy, Ellie realized she no longer could see the sun. The growth was so dense there were few shadows, and the ones there were, were shadowy themselves. She'd lost all sense of time. It seemed darker, though, and cooler. Of course, without sun filtering through, it would be, but that didn't account for all of it. Cora was struggling in her pocket. "Okay, wait a minute, Cora. Let me help you out." Ellie put her on the ground. Cora sniffed and scuttled ahead. Ellie wished she could capture Cora in this setting, especially her movements and concentration. She was mapping the piece in her head when Cora chirruped and scampered back and then darted ahead again. She chirruped again, and Ellie, finally comprehending, followed.

A half hour's walk brought them deep into a quickly darkening forest. Ellie was about to call to Cora to slow down when a blast of cold air hit her, and she quickened her pace. Cora scouted ahead, but chirruped and waited for Ellie to catch up before surging ahead again. The few times Ellie hesitated, either a chirrup from Cora or a cold blast of wind got her moving again. By the time Ellie saw the tiny hut, she was shivering. A bit shy about just entering, though, she knocked and then called out. Finally, too cold to care, she opened the door.

It was obvious no one was there or had been there in a long time. She lit a candle and saw clearly into all four corners. The hut was clean and contained only a fireplace and a long, low bench with a back like an old-fashioned pew. A worn, woolen blanket had been tossed in a pile at one end of it. Ellie secured the door. She could hear the wind drive against it. The thought occurred to her that the elevation might be high enough for it to snow tonight. It certainly felt cold enough. A good supply of kindling and small logs were stacked near the fireplace. She could have a fire now and one in the morning. She hoped Cory had found warm shelter.

After starting the fire, she turned to face the blanket. Although the cabin was clean, she didn't know if anything was hiding in the blanket, and she wanted to use it. She inspected the parts that were visible and then pulled it onto the floor by one corner and started carefully shaking it out. Cora was looking on clearly perplexed. "I don't want to wake up with a spider in my face," she explained.

Cora scratched an ear. *It's fine.* After another five minutes, Ellie herself was satisfied and spread it in front of the fire to warm. She pulled her pad and pencils out and made several quick sketches: her entry into the forest, Cora scouting, the pine trees, Cory and Connie, the wind. Finding herself yawning, Ellie decided to stop for the evening.

She was surprised at the number of sketches she had made when she quickly counted through them. She went back to the first one and studied it before flipping to the second to study it. After she'd gone through all of them, she sat and stared into the fire. She mentally reviewed her paintings and drawings from the last four years until she became too tired to think any longer. She pulled the bench nearer to the fire and, wrapping herself in the blanket, lay down and was immediately asleep.

CHAPTER 25

Cory was worrying about Ellie. He tried desperately to stop, reminding himself again that worry does nothing good. He had been hiking in the dark woods for hours, climbing over fallen logs and stumbling among tangled roots. He was bordering on being angry with God for telling Ellie to come, for separating them for the night, for leaving him without Connie, for the cold and uncomfortable night Cory knew was his. He had not been angry with God in years. It was getting darker and cold, but he sat down on a log. He had to think this through before he did or said something foolish or reckless. He put his head in his hands to concentrate.

In the year after his first engagement fell through, he had been angry with everyone. Not his parents nor his best friend, not even Connie could get through to him, and, after her first few tries, she rarely showed up. He was never mean to her, but he brushed off her offers of help. He might have even yelled at her. Why should she come around?

He started remembering those ugly times and ugly emotions. Then, he started feeling them. "I don't want to be that person again," he pleaded. He jumped up and roared, "Connie!" into the darkness, but no Connie came. Cory could feel his body vibrating. His hands were shaking, and he felt nauseated and light headed. The whole forest looked purple, not a royal purple but the purple of a bruise. "I have to calm down."

He sat and made himself breathe deeply. Little by little, the forest settled into the varying shades of dark greens and grays that dusk was turning it into. He felt his heart beat slow. His thoughts stopped whirling, and his stomach started to settle. Feeling eyes on him, he thought, Ralph? and turned slowly to be met with a pair of gold eyes belonging to a large, tawny cat. Cory swallowed hard, but her name came to him instantly, "Hello, Alexandra. I'm honored. Can you take me somewhere warm, please?" When he stood, the cat, moving alongside and pushing him to the right, herded him to a cave. Cory sighed.

He'd known earlier in the day this was where he was heading—not to this cave and with a mountain lion, but to a cave. How had he not seen the signs telling him he needed to refocus? He shook his head sadly. Berkeley had even visited. How had he not made the connection then? Thinking about where he might have gone astray, it took him a few minutes to think about the other part of that thought. Alexandra sat patiently. It was when Cory met her eyes that he thought about what he'd just said to himself: how did I miss the signs. "Oh, so that's why I was thinking about her again after all these years. Yes, I can see that now."

He had stopped just inside the cave entrance, and the wind, now frigid with the abrupt temperature drop, was making him shiver. Alexandra didn't look all that happy either. She caught his attention, turned, and sauntered deeper into the cave. Cory fumbled to get a candle lit before he lost sight of her, but, like Ralph, like all his other guides, she waited for him to catch up. As they moved deeper under the hill, the temperature moderated. Cory was still cold, but at least he wasn't shivering as much.

When they arrived in a small chamber, Cory set the candle against one wall. He unrolled the blanket and wrapped it around himself before sitting in a clear space. Alexandra came over and lay down beside him and stretched her body around one side of him and her front legs around the other. A fur afghan, thought Cory as her 101 degrees warmed him quickly. "Thank you, Alexandra," he said after a few minutes. Now warm enough, Cory pulled his pack towards him and rummaged in it for food. He offered the cat some jerky. She sniffed it but declined.

The cave was narrow, and off to his left in the flickering light, he could see that the chamber narrowed further into a passage that looked deep. He wondered if he was to go in. He hoped not. Wanting to ensure Ellie had enough candles, Cory had given her the six they had started out with and only had the remaining three from the cabin. He looked again into the murky depths. Again, he talked himself down from the emotional precipice he had been skirting all day.

Concentrating on the candle, Cory found himself being soothed and lulled by the little flame that was filling the chamber with its tiny light. This wouldn't be a bad way to spend the night, protected from the wind and cold by the cave and its furry inhabitant. Cory relaxed and thought he was dreaming when he felt Alexandra get up, but without her warmth, he soon came out of his half trance and pulled the blanket closer. He wondered where she had gone until he heard padding noises. Hoping she had brought kittens back with her, Cory looked eagerly towards the sound.

From the entrance end of the cave, came a cat larger than Alexandra and even more muscled. Cory shrank back. He thought of standing as a sign of respect but then thought that might be considered threatening. Instead, he made himself look as small and helpless as possible. That the second cat was also his evaded his conscious mind. A mad concoction of fight vs flight, terror, and panic overtook him. When the cat approached and sniffed his face and then huffed at him, he simply sat motionless and numb, his eyes huge. It took

Alexandra's licking his hand to get a reaction. Cory tried to say something, cleared his throat, and tried again. "Hi," was all that came out.

The two cats sat down in front of him and looked deep into his eyes. When he finally met their gazes, he was astonished to see blues and greens. He blinked, and their eyes again shown gold. Cory knew he should recognize the other colors as being from somewhere meaningful to him, but it was as if he'd forgotten where. As if, perhaps, he had never known, or maybe that he had known, but that they'd been taken from him, lost for a reason he could not understand.

He felt images of castles and thatched huts rise in his mind along with an ocean of stars, but he lost them, too, before he could truly grasp what they were. He looked at the larger cat, "But I want them," he whispered plaintively. He was still trying to decide if they had ever been his. The cat just sat there. Cory said more firmly, "I want them back." That got the cat's attention. Cory struggled to stand. Both cats backed up a foot or so. When Cory was standing, he looked at the larger cat and said again, "They were mine, they are mine, and I want them back." The cats were like two sphinxes. Cory crouched in front of them. The blanket fell off his shoulders as he placed a hand on each of them, "Please," he begged softly, "It was mine, and I can't remember. How could I have been so careless to lose them? Please help me get it all back. Alexandra, Hercules, please."

Hercules rose and started into the depths. Carefully picking up the candle and protecting its flame, Cory followed him. He wasn't even sure if he was supposed to. Maybe Hercules was bored or annoyed and just wanted to go somewhere by himself. Cory felt his thoughts and decided he was meant to follow. The passage narrowed but still accommodated Cory's height. The way was twisting and seemingly endless. He could see passages branching off the one they were on. He could barely keep Hercules in view and lost all sense of how long he had been following behind him.

Hurrying around a corner, Cory didn't see the outcropping. The candle was jarred from his hand and went out as it hit the stones. He could hear it roll but had no way of finding it. The darkness was complete: palpable but silent. No sound, no light, nothing reached him.

Cory froze. His heart pounded in his chest and temples. I'll be lost here forever. He turned his head. This is the way out. No, I turned around. Did I turn around? I don't think I did. He started to move one arm but quickly dropped it to his side. Don't move, he told himself. Just don't move. He forced his thoughts back to the moments before he lost the candle. It was a blank. I can't remember! He choked out a sob. When I moved my head, did I turn my body? I don't know. It was as if his blood chanted 'I don't know, I don't know' as the black blankness turned an angry red.

Cory could feel himself crumbling from the inside, his atoms separating and draining from his body. It was as if his spirit and self were splitting apart. He was gulping for air and sobbing. Before he could get even more disoriented, Cory made himself sit and breathe. He wiped his eyes on his shirt sleeve until it was drenched and no longer useful.

After a few minutes, he forced himself to go back moment by moment from when he'd dropped the candle. Had he turned around? No, he was pretty sure he had not. He forced himself to breathe more slowly. His tears slowed. Had he moved any direction? The red started to fade back to black as his head and heart lessened their pounding. He exhaled and continued. He shook his head. No, he didn't think so. Had he turned when he sat? He thought and felt. Again, the answer came back, no, he had not. Able to think more clearly now, he thought through all his movements again. Finally, he was sure he had not turned. He had only turned his head at one point and had started to move one arm, but that was all.

He let out his breath. "So, I should be facing into the depths," he said aloud. Good, he could hear his voice, but that was all he could hear, and he was shivering again. In his haste to follow Hercules, he had only brought the one, lit candle. He had not even put his jacket back on. He didn't remember taking it off. Not even any matches, he thought and laughed sadly. His eyes filled. He couldn't think past the moment and what anything might mean. So, he simply sat and let tears trickle down his face.

Hours passed through Cory's mind and then days and then years. Invisible pictures from his life passed by him and through him. He didn't want to look at them, not because he thought he was dying; he instinctively knew he wasn't. "But I am," he said. "I am dying to something, the something I'm losing, but I don't think it's my physical life." He thought of Ellie. He thought of everything they were to do. His eyes overflowed, and he wept into his hands until there were no more tears to cry. His head ached, and his eyes felt raw. He wiped them on his still-wet sleeve. And then, so simple as to be almost comical, he finally gave in.

He sat and watched and listened to the pictures and began to remember, not the green and blue yet, but he whispered, "There was white, too." He heard a huff and reached out towards the depths but could not feel anything. He was sure, though, that was Hercules' huff. Just the thought he was not alone to be lost in the cave gave him enough hope to go on. He began to remember who he was, "I'm Cory. I'm keeper of a special zoo and a guide ... and a seer," he added hesitantly.

He stopped, confused and disbelieving, but the word would not go away. If I can see the future, can I see if I get out of here? He thought about that, but nothing came. "I'm no seer," he said sadly, "but I remember." At that, he smiled and added strength to hope.

He walked again through the dream he had had in the desert. He could smell the flowers and feel the cobblestones under his feet. He reached his arms out to his sides, why he wasn't sure, but in doing so, he touched the walls of the passage. Like a concussion of thunder, everything fell back into place. If he had been standing, he would have fallen. As it was, it felt as if the floor of the cave was collapsing and that he was falling through into warmth and light. Looking with his eyes, it was still a blank darkness. Feeling with his hands, everything was still cold. *Close your eyes*, the cave whispered. Cory didn't hear at first. *Close your eyes.* This time he heard and thought of what Ellie had said about the wind. That had been just this morning. "Oh, Ellie," he sighed. "I miss you. I'm so glad you're not with me for your sake, but I so wish you were for mine." Then, obeying, Cory closed his eyes and could see.

He stood and started deeper into the cave. He smiled as he realized he'd been right earlier; he had not turned around; he was facing the cave's depths. He saw the passage open into a large chamber and saw Hercules stretched out by a pool that was green and blue. My ocean, thought Cory. I remember. That is what is green and blue. He felt the joy of remembering. He folded his legs under him and sat down by the cat. He concentrated on simply breathing and felt his heart beats—slow, steady and strong. He reached a hand into the water.

Taking his boots and socks off, he lowered his feet into the water, warm water, a hot spring. After a few moments, he stripped and lowered himself in, testing the depth. Even in the middle, it came up no farther than his shoulders. Warm again, he looked with closed eyes around the cave. It reminded him of the expanse of stars under his ocean.

Is that what I do now? I see with my eyes closed? he wondered. The inside of a cave or my own ocean doesn't seem to be something that needs to be seen except by me. He stopped. How did I almost lose them? What did I forget? He thought about that night in the desert when Ralph disappeared and he'd sat and waited and thought something similar and had asked the divine to not let him forget. But he almost had. I never again want to get close to a loss like that. "How do I keep from forgetting?" he asked, but nothing came: no thought, no perception, not even a vague impression.

Seemingly at a standstill, Cory dipped in the pool and then lazily floated on his back. Finally, feeling himself growing drowsy, he knew he should get out. He shook as much water off himself as he could before putting his clothes back on. He looked at Hercules sleeping contentedly and snuggled into the cat who started purring but did not waken.

Cory thought he would fall asleep himself, but he was oddly wide awake. In adjusting his head to get fur out of his face, he could now hear Hercules' heart. As he listened to the rhythmic beating, Cory could see through the cat's eyes. He followed a chase that ended in dinner being brought back for both cats to share. He ran and pounced. He sat on a rocky boulder and surveyed his domain. He could see through the cat's eyes and feel the cat's muscles as if they were his own. He could see into the cat's heart to the power and strength there and into the deepest depths where he protected what was his: his freedom and sense of self, his dignity and courage to go his way, to live the journey that was his and to speak his truths.

Cory pulled his thoughts out. He was shaken. He was about to deny the experience when Hercules raised his head and looked at him and into Cory's heart, and Cory knew. "I'm a mountain lion, too, aren't I? I'm to guide people not just to look past their illusions but to look into themselves and to find and to protect what is precious. That's what I see, not the future or the inside of a cave, but the inside of a person, the things inside them that can lead to their best possible futures if they are guided deep into themselves. Thank you, Hercules. I also know what I lost."

Cory sat amazed because what he had lost—the person he had been, the parts that were now of no use to him—needed to be lost. It wasn't a bad thing. It was a good thing. He hadn't needed to be afraid of the losing. "I'll not forget again who and what I truly am." The mere saying of it brought comfort.

The cat got up, yawned, stretched, and starting back down the passage, looked back once to make sure Cory was following. On the way out, Cory bent down and picked up the candle stub. Once back in the first chamber, he added it to the pouch and gathered his belongings. After thanking the cats, he headed to the cave's entrance where he was greeted by a sun just coming over the horizon and filtering through the spaces between the tree trunks.

CHAPTER 26

That he had a morning stretching out in front of him, one that was not going to be spent in a cave, did not surprise Cory in the least now. That he and Ellie would meet up by noon was assured. He could barely remember the person he had been just yesterday, the person who forgot who he was and thought he might be lost. He pondered his feelings from the last two days. Why did I need to feel them, be taken back in time to those bad years? Then he thought, what if I had not felt them? Would I have learned what I needed to?

What did I learn? The answer was immediate: I was never in danger of losing my ocean, but I must take time to reflect on my journey, let the memories change and grow, discard what is no longer useful, but always keep walking towards who I am meant to be.

I learned I'm a mountain lion. Cory paused at that and smiled as he remembered when he learned people can have helper animals. Now, to know we can be them as well, at least on a spiritual level. An image of Hank popped into his mind, and he burst out laughing: I guess I've always had the potential to be a lion. Maybe accepting and cherishing Hank all those years ago was an act of seeing into the future. At the very least, it was a foretelling of who I am now.

So, that gets me to who I am at this moment: a zoo keeper, a guide, and now a seer. Cory shook his head in wonder. To be the keeper of a very special zoo would have been enough. To also be able to guide people past their illusions to what is possible, more than enough. But to help them look inside themselves and bring out their larger knowing? And to realize many of the animals have gathered on the estate for a larger purpose? That they aren't mine just to care for but also to share, to make it possible for people to find the ones they need? He shook his head in near disbelief.

His thoughts seemed to be coming from outside himself as he continued and said aloud, "My new job is to help people bring out their raw energy and to help them make it into something useful and good." He thought a moment, "No, that's not all of it." He stopped and closed his eyes. "It's to help them change so they can become what it's always been meant for them to be. Wow, that's a lot." He opened his eyes, and then he smiled, "but I wouldn't be given this if it was impossible for me to do." Yes, he thought, the experiences of the last two days were necessary. They are to be remembered, but they aren't meant to be dwelled on. I have the blackberry pebble and the candle stub for reminders. Those are enough. Now, I have things to do.

Cory was content to walk and experience the life of the forest: the breeze that was much warmer than last night's cold wind, the sounds of hidden birds and animals. He became aware he could sense the forest growing, leaves unfurling, buds opening, babies being born. His navigation was effortless. His feet seemed dismembered from him, or, at least, they knew exactly where to place themselves without his thinking about it.

"Hi, Connie," he said at one point. *I wondered when you'd notice me.* "Have you been with me all along?" *Yes, always.* "Even in the cave?" *Of course.* "That's good to know. How did I forget?" *You were meant to forget so you can understand other people's struggles.* Cory stopped walking. "That makes a lot of sense. Thank you for explaining." *You're welcome.* "So, you've been with me in your body?" *Sort of.* "Then it wasn't a physical body.

You couldn't have flown onto my shoulder, for example." *It was the same kind of body you experienced with Hercules.* Cory could feel the truth in all of this but struggled to understand. "Can I stay in that body?" *Yes, you can stay in it and your physical body at the same time.* "I can't even begin to think about that." *You'll get used to it.* "Is that what you do?" *Not quite. It's different for totem animals.*

"I'm now a mountain lion, Connie." *You've always been one. Welcome to your realization.* "Is this how I see through its eyes?" *What do you mean?* "I kind of project into Hercules, or even Alexandra, and then leave conscious thought behind?" *Something like that. You'll get used to it and just do it. The less you think about it, the easier it is.* "It's a huge responsibility, Connie, leading people into themselves, helping them find their animals." *You'll do it.* "I hope so." *You shall.*

They talked as they had for most of Cory's life. Cory found a boulder and rested on it. Near the end of the conversation, Connie flew in and landed on his knee. "I don't understand how it works, Connie." *It just does.* "Thank you, Connie, for everything." *Of course; it's what I do.* "I'm sorry I yelled at you." *When was that?* "About eleven years ago now." *I don't remember you doing that, but if you did, it's okay. Let's go find Ellie and Cora.*

*   *   *

The night seemed days long, but Ellie stayed warm. She was sure when she awoke that the fire would be out, but the embers still glowed, and small flames still sent out their warmth and light. She was about to get up when she felt a tiny body stir. Looking down towards the crook of her knees, she saw Cora curled into a ball. She slowly freed her arms before picking the blanket up around Cora and placing them on the bench.

Ellie stoked the fire and was about to go to the door to see what kind of day awaited, but the threads of her dreams pulled her back to the bench. She laid Cora and the blanket across her lap and tried to bring back her dream images. Almost always dreaming in images and then incorporating them into her art, Ellie had no idea what to make of last night's images of shapeless colors, blocks of colors, swirls, cubes that first expanded and then became tiny and finally exploded into sparks or confetti-like particles that winked out like colored stars.

She watched the fire as the flames separated into thread-like tendrils that reached towards the mantel and then out towards her. Her conscious thought was to back up, but she intuitively reached towards them and entered them and walked among them. They seemed more than fire. The colors from her dreams divided. The warm colors joined with the fire. The cooler colors ran onto the hearth where they turned to jagged lumps like pieces of coal or untumbled rocks. She knew there was a message here, but she couldn't reach it yet.

She was reminded of her reaction to yesterday's sketches and her paintings from the last four years. The sketch of the meadow she didn't remember drawing, the one to which she'd added Cory and Connie, presented itself. She felt her love for Cory and her gratefulness to Connie for her guidance. She felt her fear from yesterday. Like a cataract, pictures paired themselves with emotions and poured through her mind. She watched the last four, then ten, then almost twenty years of pictures and feelings flash through her mind. As she reviewed earlier paintings, the emotional connections became fewer and less solid.

"That's what has been missing. That's what I'm here to learn." Her eyes became large, and she blinked several times. "I've started painting how things feel, not how I feel about them, but how they themselves feel as if I've gone inside them," she said in wonder. She put the blanket down and got her sketch pad. As she flipped through the sketches again, she could feel the emotions: Cory's, Connie's, the meadow's, the forest's, even the sun's and the wind's. But how? She thought. How can the sun feel?

That's a pretty limited view. "Good morning, Cora. It is?" *You know I feel, not just pain or cold, but excitement when I find an especially tasty tidbit and happiness when you pet me.* "Well, yes, but you're a special chipmunk." *All chipmunks feel these things.* "Okay, uh, but what about … " Ellie looked around but didn't see anything she could use. Cory's pebble came to mind.

"What about rocks?" *Oh, they feel.* Ellie thought a moment. "Do they mind when we sit on them or dig a boot in to climb up?" *No, that's their function.* "Or what about when they are carved?" *Again, that's part of what they do. When Cory kicked that rock yesterday … they don't much like that, not because it hurts, it doesn't, they're hard. They mind the energy because they have to absorb it. That too, though, is part of their job.* "Then why do they mind?" *Do you like all parts of your job?* "Well, uh, sometimes I don't feel like cleaning my brushes, but I know I have to do it." *They do, too.* "Oh," said Ellie with dawning comprehension.

She was about to ask if they should start their day when the thoughts she'd been working with didn't feel complete. She sat quietly. Cora crawled into her pocket. Ellie watched the trails of flames turn from jagged rocks and feathery tendrils back into flames that became embers that finally snuffed out and cooled. There was now enough light without them, but Ellie had closed her eyes and was surveying a night sky with its moon and stars and planets moving through. The night sky turned as if on an axis, and Ellie was looking at day with its sun and clouds and blue.

As the image rotated, she could see the night behind the day and day behind night. "They're one!" *Yes.* "Then they're not separate, the sun and moon, I mean. They're the same thing?" *On a larger scale, yes.* "How?" *Everything is part of one entirety just like you have one body but many parts.* Ellie's brow wrinkled. *How else would people be able to navigate their everyday lives if all they saw was the whole? Things on earth need reference points: young forest, meadow, old forest.* "Well, of course. Wait, you mean we wouldn't have had to come to the old forest to learn?" *Not if you had understood; you could have stayed home. Even with understanding, it's sometimes easier to take a pilgrimage.* "I can see that," said Ellie. "I can draw in a noisy place, but it's often easier in a quiet space." *Exactly.* "Sometimes the opposite is true though," remarked Ellie thoughtfully. *True too.*

Ellie's face suddenly relaxed, and, opening her eyes, she laughed aloud. "So, why paint if everything is one thing? Wait, don't tell me, Cora." She thought a moment and then said, "We need to see the differences to learn about the sameness." *That's part of it.* "So, like the pointillists, like the cubists, like any who deconstruct an object into its parts, I paint to show how everything fits together because we need them to learn, right?" *Good*, said Cora. "But, I think from now on, I will be concentrating on the emotions," continued Ellie trying to put her thoughts into words, "not just the emotional tones. Viewers won't feel just what the work seems like to them; they will feel the subject's emotions and experiences. No, that's not quite right, they will be able to see their uh, their degree, yes, degree of connection to everything else, No, wait; not 'else,' there is no else, just everything, their degree of connection to everything."

Ellie sat still before adding, "I will put the different parts together and take them apart, and I will still show what is behind, but my pictures will now be saturated with my, uh, my understanding of what is behind: that everything is not just connected, at some very high level, it's all one whole," finished Ellie, flabbergasted. *Yes*, said Cora. "And I'm part of it and have a larger purpose in my art." *Yes*, said Cora again. *I'm going to nap now.*

Ellie sat and pondered her new lessons as well as what she already knew about art, what she'd learned in classes, what she gathered from other artists. She frowned, "There's still something I'm missing." It did not want to come, and finally, she folded the blanket, put the bench back, left a small sketch for the cabin and walked outside as she hoisted her bag.

The forest had warmed. Soon, she unzipped her jacket. She sat on a rock to eat some crackers and cheese. She shared berries with Cora, who then scampered off. Looking around, Ellie wondered why she had thought the forest so terrifying before she entered it yesterday. As she looked at the trees, Ellie could sense the life in them and in the animals who lived there. She could feel their emotions, and then, more, she could feel their ... she couldn't put a word to it. Her earlier thought, and now this one, eluded her conscious mind.

"Cora?" but Cora was chasing dust motes. *She reminds me of Snickers when she was a kitten,* thought Ellie, momentarily distracted by Cora's excitement and her joy of simply being a chipmunk. "Cora?" she called again. Cora scampered up out of breath. "I won't just be painting emotions and connections." *You won't?* "No," she shook her head slowly and thought another moment before saying, "I'm not sure what I'll paint, but it will be very different from how I've been painting. I'm ready to go on. Do you want to ride in my pocket?" *No, I'm happy on the ground.*

A bit overwhelmed but accepting her new thoughts and feelings, Ellie simply wandered contentedly among the trees. The ground was smooth and flat, walking was easy and allowed her to concentrate on the life around her. Several times, Cora chirruped to suggest things Ellie might like to see and was rewarded each time with Ellie's response. The morning vanished in walking, noticing, sketching and scampering.

CHAPTER 27

Ellie was sitting on a large boulder where she had stopped to sketch a fairy ring in a small clearing when she heard Cora's excited chirrups. She quickly gathered her pencils and stuffed them and her pad into the bag before calling, "Cora?" to get a direction. Not hearing anything, she called, "Marco?" *Who's Marco?* "There you are. It's a people game when you're trying to find someone." *Come, you have to see this.* Ellie followed Cora's flitting form to an open space that was filling with emerging butterflies. Ellie did not to try to sketch. She turned in repeated circles simply taking in as much as she could to reconstruct it later.

She had to resist the temptation to help a butterfly struggling against its cocoon, but she rooted for it. *It is what it is*, said Cora coming up. "I guess so. I want it to make it though." *It may not be meant to make it.* "But, that's so sad," she said, looking closely at the cocoon and the struggle going on inside it. *Why?* "Because, uh, because … well, I don't know. We always think of death as sad, but it isn't, is it?" *Not for the one who has gone.* "But it's so much work." *What do you mean?* "It's so much work to struggle against the cocoon and then die just as it's about to be born. All that work for no reward." *No reward? It has the best reward. It joins in the wholeness of everything.* "Then why go through everything it takes to get to the point of being born? Why not just go?" Cora looked up at Ellie until Ellie looked back. *I'm going to let you think about that*, and she scampered off.

As several of the butterflies lifted in their first flights, Ellie looked across the clearing and saw Cory and Connie emerge from the underbrush. "Cory, do you see?" called Ellie.

"Yes, yes we did." Cory's face was glowing. "I'm not sure I've ever seen anything as beautiful except maybe seeing you here now," he said as he crossed the clearing. As he held her to him, he said, "It was right. Everything that happened in the last twenty-four hours was right and good." Cory released her, and they sat together on a rock. Ellie held Cory's hand as if she'd been without him for weeks and caressed his face with her eyes as if to rememorize what he looked like, but perhaps, instead, it was to try to learn how he'd changed.

Cory continued, "Before this morning, I would have said I didn't like the parts where I was cold, and it was dark, and I thought I was lost forever, and I thought Connie wasn't there, but I realize now those were some of the most meaningful parts."

Ellie suddenly understood why one must go through being born even if the actual birth doesn't happen. What she said instead was, "What do mean Connie wasn't there? You said in the meadow that she'd flown in."

Cory shook his head, "I didn't say that. I watched until you entered the forest, and then I walked across the meadow farther west."

"You couldn't have. I sat on a boulder in the meadow for I don't know how long before going in. I saw you walking towards the forest. It was after you shielded your eyes to see Cora."

Cory shook his head, "No, I was looking for Connie before you said Cora was there."

They looked at each other. "We certainly had different experiences," offered Ellie. "We wouldn't have had them had we stayed together."

They sat together quietly before Cory said, "You're right; we would have missed the most important lessons."

"I'm glad we had them. Mine were really meaningful, too, and I needed to do them alone, but I do hope we get to stay together now."

"I think we will," said Cory. "No, I know we will." He took Ellie's other hand, and they watched the butterflies: some warming themselves and drying their wings in the sunshine; others practicing their flying in swoops and flutters.

"Where do we go from here?"

"Connie and I came up from over there." Cory nodded to the southwest. "Connie, which direction? More this way?" Cory asked as he looked northwest.

Ellie looked down to get Cora's opinion. "What do you think, Cora?"

The animals seemed to be leaving it to them, so they crossed the clearing and headed northwest into an area of less densely packed trees. Ellie walked along swinging her arms and feeling joyful and free. She looked over at Cory when she heard him yawn. "Cory, honey, did you get any sleep?"

He shook his head. "No, I was up all night." When he looked back at Ellie, she could see his bleariness.

"Let's stop for a bit. You take a nap, and I'll sketch."

"I'm okay. We can keep going."

Ellie rephrased it. "I'd like to get some of the butterfly images on paper while they're fresh."

"Oh, okay." They had come to a small meadow of wildflowers and short grass. They headed to a tree where Cory lay down and was immediately asleep. Ellie folded her jacket and laid it under his head and then sat down near him. Taking out her sketch pad, she opened it to a fresh page. She took a moment to close her eyes to re-see the butterflies emerging before she started sketching. She had filled almost all the blank pages when she sensed Cory stirring.

He rolled over and, opening his eyes, yawned and stretched. "How long was I asleep?"

"Only an hour or two, I think. Feel better?"

"Much. I'm ready to go on. What do we have left to eat?"

"Not a lot. I have a few crackers and some cheese." She looked in the container. "Oh, there are also a few berries."

"I have some peanut butter and a piece of jerky. Are you hungry?"

"I'm okay." Ellie handed Cory the food she had and watched as he laid it out on the napkin he always carried on trips.

When it was neatly arranged, Cory said a blessing. "Let's finish it all off," he said to coax Ellie into helping him. When they were done, Cory pointed a direction, and they started up again. Cora had shown up in time to get the last berry and was now riding in Ellie's pocket. Connie flew in as they started and then flitted ahead. "This is how I hoped the trip would be," said Cory smiling as he took in the scene around him.

"I think it just might stay this way," agreed Ellie.

They strolled through the meadow and on into a scattering of trees before the woods grew dense again. The path was broad and even, and they pointed out things of interest: moss patterns on rocks and tree trunks, small flowers tucked under ferns, darting forms here and there. "What kind of bird is that?" asked Ellie.

Cory listened a moment to the trilling song. "I'm not sure, but I think I hear Berkeley somewhere above. He sounds satisfied." Their progress was leisurely and unhampered and remained so until late in the afternoon when they arrived at a large, bowl-like depression surrounded by dense forest.

"We could skirt it," offered Cory, pointing around to the right.

"I don't know," said Ellie, looking at the forest on both sides before peering down into the bowl. "The descent doesn't look all that steep."

As they discussed their options, Connie flew in and pointed out a path that wound down the side near where they stood. "I think it's always wisest to follow Connie."

"Agreed," said Ellie. Single file now, they walked carefully down the packed earth and loose pebbles until they stood at the bottom and gazed at the cliff sides that rose above them. Time and weather had worn the rock into natural hieroglyphs.

"This is a lot deeper than I thought it was on the way down," remarked Ellie.

Cory only nodded his agreement. He was looking around as if he knew where he was. His forehead wrinkled in concentration and he finally sighed and shook his head. "It's as if I remember this place, but it's not like yesterday when I was grasping to remember something I knew was mine and thought I'd lost. This is as if from a dream, or maybe I just think it is, and it's really from a movie. Still, it seems like a place I should know. I wonder if a meteor made it. What would you say it is? About 50 feet across?"

Ellie shrugged. "You're better at that than I am."

They studied the cliff wall for drawings. "It all seems to be natural erosion, not drawings or writings of any kind," remarked Ellie as she moved slowly to the right.

"I'm not seeing any either," said Cory from several feet away to her left.

"There's not much else either except that clump of trees at the other end."

"And a bunch of rocks," added Cory.

He pointed out a group of low rocks near the middle, and they sat.

"I don't think I told you what I learned about rocks." Ellie related what Cora had said about their function and the difference between using them to help yourself and taking out your frustration on them.

"That makes sense," replied Cory. "The energy has to go somewhere." He thought about rocks and then said, "I wish I could figure out why this place seems so familiar."

"Maybe because it's your meteor bowl?" Cory looked at her quizzically. "It's part of the estate, part of you. You may not know everything about yourself, but don't you learn more the deeper inside yourself you go?"

"Well, of course," Cory agreed. "And the experiences and learning change me, and I, in turn, change the experiences."

Ellie looked lovingly at him. "And that's why it was given to you to keep the helper animals, Cory."

He blushed but said, "Yes, and now I'm a seer and mountain lion, too."

Ellie nodded and smiled, glad he'd decided to claim them.

"Which way now?"

"I think continuing in the direction we were heading before we got to this bowl makes sense except the cliff at the far end looks really steep. Do you think we should go back to where we entered and go up and around like you suggested earlier?" asked Ellie. "It's almost all rock ahead and higher too. Where we came in is lower and has that path."

Cory looked back at the mix of dirt and rocks and then ahead. "Let's explore a bit more closely ahead," he said nodding to the rock wall and clump of trees, "and then decide. It may be easier than it looks from here. We can always backtrack."

They hoisted their bags and started towards the far end. When they approached the rock face, they searched for a path. Connie apparently had decided to let them do this one on their own, and Cora had scampered off somewhere. Making their way around behind the trees, they stopped in amazement and looked at each other.

"You're smiling like the cat that ate the canary," said Cory.

"You are, too," replied Ellie. "Why didn't we notice this earlier?"

"We only looked from a distance. We didn't come this far."

Hewn into the base of the cliff was a door-sized opening; moreover, they could see steps. They each lit a candle and entered.

CHAPTER 28

The steps progressed in a smooth flow upward until they emerged into a small area cleared of trees. As they looked around to get their bearings, they could just make out what seemed to be the remains of an ancient building in front of them, perhaps an open courtyard as there were no walls or even rubble, suggesting walls had never existed.

"I think it's a temple," whispered Cory. Ellie just nodded her agreement. They looked back. The thick stand of trees and underbrush behind them hid the bowl from view and hid the temple until a person was standing where they were now. Even with being just a few yards away, they could have missed it and walked on by. Because of its vine and creeper covering, it was almost unrecognizable.

"Did you have any idea this was here?" asked Ellie

"No. It always amazes me the things I find on the estate." They simply stood and gazed.

"Look." Ellie was pointing up. At first, Cory thought she meant the sky. Slowly, his perceptions took on meaning, and he realized she was pointing at the trees from which a long row of pillars was made. The trunks were so covered now in vines it was difficult to make them out as pillars except by looking upward to foliage at the top where one could follow the lines of the trunks down to the ground. The pillars seemed to mark the edge of the entire temple, but those down the sides faded into the rest of the forest. If there were pillars at the far end, it was impossible to see from where they were standing.

"What a marvelous discovery," he whispered. Ellie nodded. "You want to sketch?" She shook her head. Birds flitted among the trunks and rested in the foliage. They heard the same trilling song they'd heard earlier in the day. They ventured through a double row of flowering bushes down a broad path that seemed to be the approach to the temple. At first of packed dirt, the path soon became cobblestones and then flagstones. At the temple's entrance, the threshold, between two closely set pillars, was one solid, flat rock.

Inside the row of tree pillars was a second row. These were of stone, hewn and stacked. The stone pillars seemed only to be on the side in front of them as if to designate this as the main entrance. Beyond them, a large courtyard had been fashioned, open to the sky but somewhat protected by the overhanging tree branches and bounded loosely on the sides by rocks and bushes. What lay at the temple's farther end, they still had no idea as dense branches and undergrowth obscured the view there, also.

The floor of the temple was clean, presumably swept by the wind and scrubbed by pine needles. They became aware of rustling sounds and bird songs other than the trilling, which they could still hear. Peering closely into the branches, they saw birds' nests, dozens of them, maybe hundreds. As if from a signal, birds began flitting from tree to tree above them. More and more joined in. Soon they were swooping in a ring above, around and around as if in a choreographed dance.

"It's like the butterflies this morning," said Ellie in wonder. Cory just nodded. After several minutes, the birds returned to their respective nests and became quiet except for the one bird's soft trilling. A warm, gentle breeze flowed around them. Cory and Ellie became aware that the courtyard was not completely empty. As they strolled around looking at everything, they could make out a depression near the center. From even a few yards away, the texture and patterns of the stone pavers hid it. Looking down into it from near its rim, though, they could see that it was shallow and only about ten to fifteen feet across. A table had been laid with a dozen or so plates of different foods. Ellie looked questioningly at Cory.

"It's for us," he said. When she hesitated, he added, "like the food at the ocean when we met."

"Oh, I guess I thought you'd brought that with you from your house, but you couldn't have," she added as Cory descended and held out a hand to her. "You didn't know then you had an ocean so close."

"Like this temple, I didn't have a clue I had one at all," he said as he held tightly to Ellie's hand as she descended. He knew she could make it down the steps safely on her own, and there were only five, but he liked doing it.

"What does that mean when you, and by that I mean anyone, when you don't know you have something like this?"

Cory thought a moment. "I think it can mean different things all at the same time."

"Such as?" she asked as she looked over the offerings on the table.

"I think it can mean the person's untapped potential as well as worn-out habits that need to be shed, also blessings as yet unclaimed, and old ideas that need to be discarded." Cory shrugged as Ellie turned to him.

"Yes, I can see that," she responded thoughtfully. "Maybe they are also new ideas, ideas that know if they presented themselves at a different time, they would be discarded, or at least set aside, so they wait to present themselves when we're ready to accept them."

Cory's whole body jolted with his sudden realization. Ellie hadn't noticed, so he didn't say anything except, "We haven't eaten much in the last two days. Let's enjoy what's here." The dishes held various kinds of berries; sweet, plain, and sourdough breads; cheeses ranging from mild to pungent; and a bowl of mixed grapes and melon slices. Several tiny saucers held salt, spices and herbs. A pitcher of water and two earthenware cups stood to one side. Beside them were finger bowls and towels. They washed their hands and slid onto the bench that was set against the rock wall.

"What a feast," sighed Ellie contentedly as they were eating the last bites.

"I think there's one more course," said Cory.

"Where?" asked Ellie looking around the table.

Cory waited until she looked at him. When she did, she blushed. The look on his face was of such adoration. He gently took her hand and kissed her fingers. "At the altar. If I'm correct, a commitment ceremony has been set for us at the far end of the temple."

Ellie smiled into his eyes. "Oh, my dearest, I think that's perfect. I'm ready."

They walked hand in hand towards the far end of the temple where they saw an altar, the top of which had been hewn from the same rock as the temple. It had been fitted between two trees and rested on stumps that provided the base. The trees must have been young when the altar was placed between them because their trunks had grown over the ends of the top and their lowest branches wound around the stumps and the top's edge. Nothing was on the altar except two coronets of flowers. No person appeared to tell them what to do, but when Cory heard padding noises, he put his arm around Ellie. "I think Hercules and Alexandra are joining us." The two cats strolled in and sat down flanking them.

Cory thought Ellie might flinch at the size and power of the cats, but she put her hand on Alexandra. "I can feel her purring. Oh, I can also feel what I'm supposed to do," she said as she reached for a laurel wreath entwined with roses and placed it on Cory's head.

Cory started to reach out to Hercules and then realized he didn't need to. He turned towards Ellie and placed the twin to his wreath on her head. He then offered her his hands, which she gladly accepted. Cory rubbed his thumb over her wedding ring and remembered how she'd insisted on a simple band because anything she wore would get paint on it. Then, he began.

"I, Cory Waters, helper of totem animals, guide, seer, and mountain lion do solemnly swear my undying love and devotion both to you throughout eternity and to our work on this earthly plane of existence as long as we are here. I promise to grow and become as it has been written for me to do so."

"I Ellie Sanborn-Waters, an artist, teacher, and painter of things as they truly are return that love and devotion and promise my support and help to you and to our earthly work. I, too, promise to claim my destiny and become what it has always intended for me to be."

The cats rose and led them on either side of the alter to where they reunited. There was a short wait until Cora and Connie joined them. Connie lit on Cory's outer shoulder. Ellie scooped up Cora who climbed into her pocket. "Cora," Ellie whispered to her as they walked. "I won't just be painting emotions." *You won't?* "No," she shook her head slowly and thought another moment before saying, "I will paint energy: the spirits of things, animals, people, places." *That's a lot of energy. How will you choose?* Ellie turned to her. "Oh, I won't choose. What I paint will tell me which energies to include." *Wise decision.*

Birds gathered and preceded their approach to the far end of the temple where they all passed through a row of tree pillars and out a small opening between two of them to the edge of a meadow, only an hour or so from Ellie and Cory's house. Before emerging from the old forest into the golden light of the meadow, they placed their coronets on Hercules and Alexandra. The cats stayed in the shadows. The birds circled back to their nests. Taking their place and following behind Cory and Ellie like the train of a wedding veil or a christening gown were the hundreds of butterflies that had also emerged that afternoon. Looking back, Cory and Ellie could see the cats like decorated sphinxes guarding their progress.

"I'm sorry. What did you just say?" asked Ellie as they strolled through the meadow.

"I didn't say anything," responded Cory.

"Ah, it was the wind, then."

"What did it say?"

Everything is and always has been as it should be.

CHAPTER 29

Back home, Ellie went into her studio and set up three easels. She placed a small canvas on the easel to the left. To its right, she set a large canvas across the other two easels. Cory watched from the doorway. When Ellie felt his presence, he said. "I thought you were only going to paint the one of the butterfly that made it home."

"I was, but I remembered what you said about making a composite of a group of small drawings." As she explained, she tacked the last three days' sketches around the large canvas, changing positions of some, tearing others in half or marking them with "Ellieglyphics," as Cory called the cues she jotted to remind herself what sketches meant or where they were to be placed. Cory kissed her hair and said he was going to go see Ralph. "Okay," she replied vaguely.

Cory wrapped a piece of cheese in waxed paper, but, before heading to the desert, he strolled over to the Japanese bridge and then, seeing Berkeley, took the shortcut and arrived at the spring just after the hawk. They walked around to the right. The little pool had expanded, more than doubling. Cory could see through its depths to the forest beneath and on to the nothingness that is everything and is home. "Thank you, Berkeley," he said. "I'll pay better attention from now on." *But by going, you were able to meet Hercules and Alexandra. We especially wanted that to happen.* "Yes, I'm glad that happened, too." Berkeley cocked his head at him. "Is there anything I can do for you, Berkeley?" *Just keep doing what you know to do and learn.*

"Thank you. I will." *I'll be around.* Cory nodded and made room for his take off.

*   *   *

Ellie worked solidly for months. After the paintings were finished, they invited Michel to come view them. Cory helped Ellie strip the studio of anything that could distract from the two canvases. When Michel arrived, she had him enter first. He walked up to the canvases and seemed to freeze in place. He stood for so long that Ellie brought him a stool. He put a hand on it to get his bearings and then sat for more than a half hour.

Finally, he tore his gaze from the canvases and looking at Ellie and Cory said, "What am I to say? I can feel that little one's death. It hoped to live, to fly, but it realizes it won't be a butterfly." Michel added no other observations. Ellie bit the inside of her mouth to keep herself from saying anything. She had thought she'd also captured its other knowing, but she had obviously failed.

Michel then turned to the larger canvas. Ellie had left the sketches. "You have never painted from a process like this, have you? I don't mean using the sketches as notes. I mean the deconstruction and reconstruction."

She shook her head, "No, you're right. I haven't."

"It's brilliant. The canvas tells a story. No, more than that. It's a map of how to get from here," he pointed to the upper left corner, "to here." He moved his finger to a midpoint at the right edge. Leaving his finger in place, he looked back to the left and then through the painting as if searching for something.

"You are very clever," he whispered. When he looked at her, Ellie could see tears in his eyes. "This shows how we become, how we shed bitterness" he pointed, "and fear and anger and get to hope and knowledge and love." At each word, he pointed to something different in the painting. Ellie hadn't noticed when she planned the painting that the progression was like a map that started in despair and ended in... Michel asked, "The little butterfly did make it, didn't he?"

"I'm not following, Michel."

He pointed to the smaller canvas. "He may not become a butterfly, but he knows he's going home." She nodded and bit her lip this time to keep from crying. She had succeeded after all.

Michel arranged to have both canvases taken to his gallery. Even before the formal showing, they were bought by a private collector who, after the gallery show, put them on permanent loan to his favorite museum.

Weeks later, Ellie walked into Cory's study. He was putting the pouch away. "I never asked if you found any mementos while we were separated."

"Just the candle stub," he said. "I didn't need any others. I wondered at the time, especially when we left the coronets in the forest, but I later realized your paintings are enough. They are remembrances for everyone who sees them."

"Wow," said Ellie as she leaned against the door jam. "I believe that's the nicest compliment I've ever received about anything."

"Better than being shown in a major museum?"

"Much better. A museum just provides the needed exposure."

CHAPTER 30

Over the years, Cory and Ellie made a number of trips to the old-growth forest, sometimes when they just wanted to enjoy its depths, but especially when their practical responsibilities felt too weighty. Occasionally, Connie or Cora went with them, but mostly they went alone to meet Alexandra and Hercules and wander the paths, visit the cabin and the cave, sit on the rocks and thank them, and leave little gifts for the spirits that reside throughout the forest.

They often visited the butterfly clearing but never again were witness to a birthing. Then again, they could still see it if they closed their eyes. Besides, they had the many generations of butterflies who now made their home on the little island. Accessible by the bridge, the island became Cory's second go-to place. He and Ellie visited often, and Cory regularly took visitors there to learn and to work on becoming. Mostly though, they and the world had Ellie's paintings, *Emergence* and *Home*.

And, throughout the desert, the ocean, the meadows and the forests, the animals went about their business. The Zookeeper smiled.

ABOUT THE AUTHOR

I have had many lives: high school English and mathematics teacher, university psychology lecturer, loan representative, retail associate, college administrator. I have written and kept journals much of my life, beginning with dream journals as a teenager. I am passionate about finding beauty in the world: in people and nature as well as in what people create, but mostly in people themselves. I hope my story will encourage you on your spiritual journey of becoming.

Find more stories and poetry at
www.StoryGiverLLC.com

46355551R00108

Made in the USA
Middletown, DE
29 July 2017